Sing Me HOME

Shannon O'Brien

BELLA
BOOKS

2016

About the Author

Shannon O'Brien is a proud Pennsylvanian, although she wrote this novel while living in Dublin, Ireland. She spends most of her time as a Props Master and Set Designer for various theatre companies and productions around the world. Her last time writing an 'About the Author' blurb was for a stage prop at the Walnut Street Theatre in Philadelphia. That one was considerably easier.

Dedication

For Susan Romano O'Brien

A woman who never failed to encourage, inspire, and buy all

the books I ever wanted to read.

and

Yes, Da, you can be my red carpet date if this book wins any

awards.

Acknowledgments

Thanks must go where they are due. This novel would not have been possible without the help and support of Becca Muskat, who took copious notes on her phone while we outlined this series one sunny afternoon in the Gardens (both Longwood and Olive). Smith College gave me an education, in more ways than I thought possible. The female-centered environment of this story sprung from my years growing in Cutter House surrounded by amazing women from all walks of life: Perri (and Lisa!), Melinda, Kirstie, Christina, Nicole, Julia, Jane, the unrelenting and overworked theatre majors and all the others that I met on the way. Thank you for growing with me. Thanks to the real life Mo, who made 18A a home, as well as my other Irish loved ones who made me never want to leave: Sarah, Imelda, David, Natasha and Dave Rudden. Thanks to Kyle for supporting me through revision after revision and for listening to me complain quite a bit. A special thank you to Jackie and Shelly, of Crossfield Writers, for walking me through the editing process from start to finish and for helping me to understand that gerunds are not my friend. Also, many thanks to my perpetually proofreading father and Miss Laura, who helped to encourage me each Sunday morning as they listened to me rant from half a world away. Finally, to Crapapella, for teaching me that sometimes failure is the best (and most exciting) outcome.

CHAPTER ONE

Stop watching the clock.

Ellie closed her eyes to force her thoughts elsewhere. Another long shift at the café only added to her stress level. Luckily, she was only twenty minutes away from kicking the late-night stragglers out and closing down for the night. The downside about working part-time at the coffee joint on campus was that all the insomniacs and night owls loved to camp out and keep her from getting ahead of her cleaning duties.

She opened her eyes again to check on her regulars. The girl with the bandana was typing away furiously, apparently struck by a rare moment of inspiration. Two booths down, the Ellen DeGeneres look-alike had closed her book to text someone. Across the room, the redhead hipster peacefully sipped her third cappuccino of the night.

Ellie sighed and began the long process of emptying the coffee dispensers, a mindless process that provided her with ample time for worry. Her final year at Jones University, an all-female college in the small town of East Westwick, was proving to be the most difficult yet. Between the maximum number of shifts allowed at the café, her packed class schedule, and the hours of a cappella rehearsal each week, Ellie barely managed to find time for her friends. It was already the middle of October, and she felt her long-awaited senior year slipping through her fingers. There was nothing she could do to stop it. She couldn't drop any courses or she wouldn't be able to graduate in the spring. Fewer shifts at the café were also out of the question; after graduation, she faced student loans. And a cappella was the only real joy she had left. Her daily planner was marked in a whole rainbow of colors, but she always saved purple, her favorite, for the music-related activities. Singing with the Jones Tones and being their treasurer was a dream come true, even if there was a bit more drama than Ellie would have liked. She looked forward to rehearsals and felt her heart race each time the group got up on stage to perform. She found herself wondering what life would be like after graduation when she didn't have the built-in support system of a cappella to sustain her. Ellie quickly steered her thoughts away from that painful idea and set the first coffee dispenser on the rack to dry. She eyed the customers again before a commotion in the back room startled her.

Rose sped out from around the corner that led to the kitchen, holding her oversized travel mug out expectantly.

"Wait, girl! I need my last refill before my long trek home," Rose exclaimed. She shoved the mug under Ellie's nose.

Ellie rolled her eyes. "You live closer than I do," she complained.

Rose sighed tiredly. "That may be true, but my knees are at least fifteen years older than yours, so it feels like miles and miles to go before I get to sleep."

As Rose poured the dregs of the hazelnut roast into her mug, Ellie felt a rush of affection. There was something comforting about having a boss like Rose around during the late-night shifts. She was a wonderful supervisor, just enough of a hard-ass to keep everyone motivated, but still happy to chat about the latest campus gossip. Rose had graduated from Jones just after the millennium, but had never moved on from East Westwick.

Sometimes, Ellie wondered what kept her in the small college town. It definitely wasn't the coffee or the paycheck she got from the café.

"Don't forget, your books are on my desk." Rose took a long drink from her mug. "Wouldn't want to give you an excuse for not doing your homework on time."

"Funny. You know very well that I do all my homework on time," Ellie answered, lifting another container into the shallow sink. She glanced at Rose, now perched on a stool next to the register, and was met by a skeptical look.

"Okay. Most of the time," Ellie admitted.

Rose blinked. "Uh-huh. Sure."

Ellie loved her boss's no-nonsense attitude. "God, you know me too well. I need to cut back on my shifts."

This elicited a belly laugh from Rose. "No can do, sweet cheeks. You're my best worker. I'm already getting panicky thinking about what I'm going to do when you leave me." She grimaced. "Why do I even remind myself?"

Ellie was flattered. It felt nice to be appreciated for all the crappy jobs she did in the café. Being a barista wasn't her calling in life, but she was grateful that she could always fall back on it, if need be.

As Rose made her rounds to remind customers that it was time to leave, most seemed surprised that it was already midnight. Ellie understood how they felt. She still had at least thirty more minutes of cleanup and an assignment to do before she went to bed. Fortunately, her first class wasn't until ten thirty, so she had a little wiggle room with the homework situation. Rose locked the glass doors behind the DeGeneres look-alike and circled back to the counter.

"Pass me the rag and spray bottle. I'll do table duty," Rose said as she placed her coffee aside.

Ellie handed over the items. "Oh! I just remembered," she said. "I'll be a few minutes late for my shift tomorrow. My class is doing a group project thing and we're supposed to split up to discuss topics after class. I already told Xiaoli that I owe her a snack or something for staying late to cover for me."

"Not a problem," Rose said as she began flipping chairs upside down. "But you owe me a snack too."

Ellie chuckled. "And what type of snack do you need to forget about my unforgivable infraction?"

"I prefer payment in beer. Or Oreos. Your choice."

Ellie nodded, noting that she needed to swipe some Oreos from a friend in her dorm before class tomorrow. In less than thirty minutes, the shop was clean and closed—record time for a Wednesday evening. As they turned off the lights and headed out the back door, Rose took another sip of coffee.

"So, what class is stealing you away from me tomorrow?" she asked, steam rolling from between her lips.

"Women in Politics. It's a SWaG class." Ellie buttoned her coat, already weary of the cold.

"Ah, yes. The good ole Study of Women and Gender Department. Well, I guess I approve. You do know how I like to study women."

Ellie laughed at the bad joke. "Wow. I've never heard that one before."

"That's your punishment for being a SWaG minor. You have to appreciate my jokes, or else."

They headed for the only traffic light on campus. "Any jokes about Museum Studies majors?" Ellie asked with a grin.

Rose beamed. "Oh, loads!"

"Go on. Tell me one." Ellie looked at her boss expectantly.

Rose thought for a second, and then looked at Ellie with a mischievous glint in her eye. "I'll tell you on your last day of work."

Ellie frowned. "It must be a really bad joke. Am I not going to want to talk to you again after you tell it?"

"Something like that," Rose said as she turned toward her apartment. "I'll see you tomorrow, girl!"

As she waited for the crosswalk light to change, Ellie's thoughts turned to the homework shoved hastily into her backpack. It was another long night in the making, but she was at least excited for something new in her SWaG class.

CHAPTER TWO

Get your sorry ass out of bed.

Jolene rolled over to slap at her phone. The soulful voice of Dolly Parton singing her namesake song was no match for the need to get more rest. Unfortunately, she had forgotten to close the dusty blinds before she collapsed into bed the night before. The harsh sunlight on her pillow was even more annoying than the alarm. She didn't want to lift her head off the very warm and comfortable pillow just yet.

After pressing snooze two more times, Jolene pushed back her comforter with annoyance. Since the beginning of the semester, her energy had left her completely. She was sure it was due to her quickly approaching graduation date. Unlike many of her friends, Jolene would don her cap and gown in the winter. She had worked tirelessly to get all the credits necessary to receive her diploma a semester early, but the thought of missing all the traditions that accompanied spring graduation made her even more sullen.

She was lucky to graduate early. It meant fewer bills to pay and a head start in the job market. But, at the same time, she would leave behind some of her greatest friends and the school she loved. As Jolene headed to the shower, she passed by a first-year student leaving for class. It made her miss those not-too-distant days. She thought of how easy college had been when she had been a new student at Jones. The poor girl probably didn't realize yet how good she had it. Jolene shook herself from thoughts of the past. She stepped under the spray of disappointing water pressure and mentally prepared for the day ahead of her.

First was class at ten thirty with Professor Mehra. Then she had a break for lunch, probably on her own since her friends were usually busy on Thursdays. After that was a Political Science class at one ten and her seminar at three. And, of course, after dinner was rehearsal.

Back in the comfort of her dorm room, Jolene toweled off and checked her planner for any overlooked homework for her morning class. 'SWaG 302: Women in Politics' was offered only once every other year, which helped to make it the most popular class in the Study of Women and Gender Department. Unfortunately, Jolene found herself more disconnected from the subject than ever. She loved the heated discussions, but couldn't muster the strength to participate anymore. She felt the 'senior slide' getting worse each day and she couldn't figure out how to fix it.

Jolene sighed when she saw the assignment written in smudged ink. She had forgotten all about the fifty-page reading assignment. Hopefully, Professor Mehra wouldn't split them up into small discussion groups. It was always so obvious when someone was bullshitting, and when it happened to her, she felt so useless. Letting herself down was okay, but letting down other students who were actively trying to learn was a different story.

As she pulled on a sock, Jolene considered skipping the class but realized that it would make her third unexcused absence. She also knew about Professor Mehra's "three strikes" policy and decided to ignore her impulse. Jolene pulled on the other sock. It was her last semester, after all. Pretty soon she would be wishing for the days when her schedule had been planned out from morning to midnight. She glanced at the clock.

"Shit."

The breakfast bar closed in five minutes. She grabbed her backpack, earphones and the unread packet. She could at least skim it before class. Skimming helped, if only a little.

The sound of her thick leather boots echoed through the stairwell as she sprinted down the stairs. It wasn't pretty, but she was determined to get some food. As she rounded the corner into the dining hall, she saw her friends at their usual table. Jolene grabbed a muffin and some fruit on her way over.

"Hey guys."

"Good morning sunshine," Natalie answered happily. She seemed ready for the start of her day, her breakfast dishes empty except for a few crumbs, and absorbed in a heavy book cradled in her lap. Her bright red hair reflected the early morning sun streaming in through the skylights. In her four years at Jones, Jolene had never seen Natalie's hair in a ponytail. She admired her for always taking time at night to put her hair in curlers so it would look perfect every day, even if she didn't quite understand the appeal of all that work. These days, Jolene felt lucky if she could get her hair washed. Most of the time, she just braided and forgot it, caught up with weightier thoughts.

"Natalie's a little preoccupied this morning," Mo explained.

Mo was still in her pajamas and bathrobe, her hair a mess of tangles and yesterday's makeup still smudged across her skin. Despite being ambitious about her studies, Mo had organized her class schedule to have no morning classes on Tuesdays or Thursdays. Twice a week, she watched smugly and with a disheveled appearance as Jolene and Natalie trudged to class after a quick breakfast. She, on the other hand, had the morning free to do whatever she wanted. Most times, she went back upstairs to bed.

"I was up all night. These last few chapters have been all cliffhanger. I couldn't stop," Natalie murmured, eyes fixed on the page.

Jolene laughed into her bite of apple as Mo shook her head.

"Always with the reading!" Mo whined.

Jolene opened her own assignment. "She *is* an English major," she offered.

"Oh, is it contagious? Are you one now too?" Mo asked, pointing at Jolene's homework.

From across the table, Natalie gave a quiet laugh.

"Believe me, I'd be the worst English major."

"Yeah, I believe you," Natalie answered.

Jolene feigned hurt but couldn't stop her lips from curving upward when she saw Natalie's sideways glance up from the page.

"Well, if you two are just going to waste this precious time that we have together with homework, I'm going to go back upstairs with my bagel." Mo frowned dramatically. Jolene frequently wondered why Mo even got up for breakfast with them, since she and Natalie often used the time for last-minute assignments. She knew that the answer was probably something sappy like "friendship" or "camaraderie." Of their trio, Mo was by far the most sensitive. She even had a saying about how you couldn't have e*mo*tions without Mo, which always made them groan. Jolene usually shrugged off overly dramatic displays of affection but, if she was totally honest, she was grateful to have both of these women as her friends and constant support.

"See you at dinner?" Jolene asked as Mo moved her bagel onto a napkin.

"No! I'll be too busy reading," Mo answered with smug look. Natalie chuckled.

"Really?" Jolene turned her best puppy dog eyes toward Mo. Mo sighed. "Of course I'll be here. I manage my time correctly, so I don't have to multitask while I eat," she explained, whipping her bathrobe like a cloak as she exited.

"See you tonight!" Jolene called, happy to see Mo's slender fingers wave goodbye as she disappeared through the doorway.

"Finally, some peace and quiet," Natalie exhaled.

Jolene looked at the reading assignment before her. She didn't have much time to skim.

CHAPTER THREE

I can't believe she took my seat.

Ellie sighed as she looked around the room. The only sophomore in class had taken her usual seat by the window in the second row. Overeager beaver. How had a sophomore even managed to get approval for a three hundred-level class? Reluctantly, Ellie parked herself in the only open window seat in the last row of the small lecture hall. As she unloaded her bag, Ellie went through her mental checklist: pen, reading packet, planner and tea. Everything was accounted for so she took a minute to relax and sip her drink.

She watched the front of the classroom while the last few dawdlers meandered toward their seats. Her usual seat in the second row never gave her this vantage point. She was struck by the number of tired-looking students in the room. Only two months into the semester and people already looked like they were falling apart. Ellie completely understood. Sometimes, she thought she wouldn't be able to make it either. Professor Mehra strode in at ten thirty on the dot, looking as regal as ever with a perfectly tailored pantsuit and a cozy-looking shawl draped elegantly over her shoulders. Ellie had to admit that she was a little bit in love with her professor. Everyone who had ever laid eyes on her had to agree that she was a fox, but it was mostly her intellect that had countless undergrads waiting outside her office for advice each week during office hours.

Professor Mehra circulated the attendance sheet as she began her lecture. "Good morning everyone. I hope you all read the assignment since we will be discussing it thoroughly today. I don't like to play favorites but"—her eyes twinkled—"I will admit that this piece holds a special place in my heart. So, let's get…"

Ellie's attention was drawn away from her professor as a straggling classmate slowly made her way into the room. The student had clearly mastered the nonchalant-cool-girl routine. Ellie recognized her, even behind the aviators and oversized beanie. Jolene Weiss was a legend in certain social circles at Jones University, especially a cappella circles. She was one of the most popular members of Acapellago, one of the four groups on campus. Ellie had always been jealous of the group, especially since they had turned her down when she auditioned as a first-year student just trying to break into the a cappella scene on campus. Luckily, the Jones Tones had seen Ellie's potential and taken her in that same year. She had moved up in the ranks and now enjoyed being one of the group's main players. Unsurprisingly, being a senior had its perks.

Ellie watched as Jolene quietly made her way to the back of the room and slipped into an empty desk two seats over from Ellie. Shrewdly, she sat down just ahead of the sign-in sheet's current location, scribbled her name on the clipboard, and passed it across the empty desk between them. Ellie picked up the clipboard with a wary look as Jolene paused her music and took out her earbuds. The girl had a flair for the dramatic, but the tardiness was still pretty pathetic in Ellie's opinion.

Ellie concentrated on Professor Mehra, to catch what she had missed while she had been distracted, "—should spend some time unpacking the reading before we really start discussing the larger issues presented. Please pair off in groups of two or three and take the next"—she glanced at the clock—"ten minutes to get the ball rolling."

Murmurs spread throughout the room as classmates paired off. Being stuck in the corner, Ellie had only one option.

She swiveled her seat toward Jolene. "Hey. Should we pair off for this?"

Jolene glanced up distractedly. "Uh. Yeah. That sounds good."

Ellie decided to take the lead and leaned in closer. "So, where do you want to start?"

"Well, what did you think of it?" Jolene asked as she flipped through the article in front of her. Ellie noticed there were no notes scrawled in the margins or highlighted passages anywhere on the pages. That was a bad sign.

"The article?" Ellie asked, flipping through her own packet, which was marked in a variety of colors.

Jolene nodded.

"Well, I read the whole thing without noticing the publication date." Ellie wondered whether her partner had even bothered to read it. She often questioned how 'cool girls' even managed to graduate.

"Oh?"

Ellie looked down at the title page. "Yeah. December 1978. So, that changed my entire stance on the article."

"How so?" Jolene asked, eyes averted.

The conversation was like pulling teeth. Ellie watched Professor Mehra ghost her way around the room, listening in on conversations as she passed by. Unlike her partner, she could at least prove that she had been ready for class.

"Well, the whole thing is pointing out how much things are changing for women in public office. There are multiple citations of a rise in representation for women throughout the United States," Ellie said crisply. "I mean, she discusses Hawaii as this hotbed of sexual equalization in politics, but we are seeing this article through a different lens than when she wrote it. I was disappointed because so little has really changed since then." Ellie was pleased with her articulation of what bothered her about the reading and glanced at her notes again to see what else she could say to impress Professor Mehra.

Jolene flipped through the article. "That's a good point, but I think you're a little too harsh," she answered.

So, her partner had a stance after all. "Okay. Tell me what you think."

Jolene responded without hesitation. "First off, we have to admit that Hawaii was, and still is, a heavily Democratic state. It's only gone red in two presidential elections in the last fifty years. On top of that, they recently elected their first ever female senator. Her name is Mazie Hirono, and she also happens to be one of only three Buddhist senators and the first Asian-American woman elected to the senate. So, taking all that into account, we know that the article was certainly correct in predicting that Hawaii would continue to be a place where women could enter the political sphere. Instead of faulting the author for writing something rooted in a time when feminism was only just sprouting wings, I think we should commend her for predicting which of the fifty states would become the most diverse, both in gender and race, for women in politics."

Professor Mehra hovered nearby, nodding in agreement. Ellie was aghast. How had Jolene listed off all that information without any notes? At least there was one glaring flaw in the argument she had just posed.

"Well, I suppose you're right. But, I think you know better than to say that feminism started in the 1970s," she chided.

Their eyes met for the first time and Jolene immediately smiled. It was different than that first grin she had seen when Jolene snuck into the seat just in time to write her name on the attendance sheet. Ellie was caught between feeling extremely jealous of Jolene's easy negotiation of the reading assignment and a simmer of something else she couldn't quite explain. She felt her cheeks warm.

Jolene quickly schooled her features into one of complete seriousness. "How could I be so silly? They teach us Feminism 101 on the first day of orientation!"

Ellie chuckled and lowered her gaze to the desktop. "So, I guess you're into politics, then."

"Yeah. American Studies major with a concentration in politics."

That explained things. Ellie examined her marked margins and nodded. "Wow. Then this article is right up your alley, I guess."

Jolene paused. "To be honest, I didn't even read the whole thing. I skimmed the first two pages over breakfast this morning."

Ellie looked at Jolene to see whether she was joking, but decided she was not.

"Oh my god! Come on! I can't believe you BS'd that in front of Professor Mehra and she still gave you the silent nod of encouragement. You suck," Ellie protested, moping over how much time she had put into the homework for this class after her late-night shift.

Jolene laughed.

"All right ladies. Let's reconvene," Professor Mehra announced as she made her way back to the front of the room.

She opened the discussion to students, asking them to support their opinions with examples from history. One student mentioned Leslie Knope as an example of the changing role of women in politics. Ellie caught a glimpse of Jolene shaking her head at that comment. She suppressed a giggle and quickly turned her attention back to the front of the room. Professor Mehra asked Jolene to repeat the observations she had made during the breakout session. Jolene rattled off the facts about modern politics in Hawaii again, proving to Ellie that she really did have an insight into women in politics and she hadn't needed the assigned reading to get there. Ellie took notes until her hand ached. If she had learned anything from talking with students that had taken a class with Mehra, it was that you never knew what topics she would touch on in the final.

Professor Mehra thanked a student for her comment and grabbed a paper off the podium. "I hope you all remembered to read the syllabus. I need you all to stay a few extra minutes today to pair off in groups of two for your midterm project." She looked down at the attendance sheet, "Thankfully, we're all present today, so no worries there. I will need you to hand in a thesis statement at the beginning of class on Tuesday. So, exchange emails or set a time to get together with your partner. If you are a little fuzzy on details, there is a full description of what this project entails in your syllabus. I also have office hours tomorrow if you need more clarification. All right"—she paused to look around the room once—"go find your partner!"

Jolene was already packed up, with her beanie on and earbuds hanging around her neck.

"Partners?" Jolene asked.

Ellie hesitated. "Only if you do the reading."

Jolene laughed. "Deal," she replied.

Ellie opened her planner and looked over her schedule for the week. "When are you free to meet?"

"Well, I have rehearsal tonight."

Ellie knew that. She had her own rehearsal too. All four of the a cappella groups on campus rehearsed on Thursday nights. Did Jolene not recognize her from the annual events when all the groups sang together?

"How about Saturday afternoon?" Jolene suggested.

"Yeah. That'll work for me. Two o'clock in the Campus Center café?"

"Sounds perfect," Jolene agreed.

Jolene didn't write down the date or time; all her books were already in the bag at her feet.

"Are you going to remember that?" Ellie demanded.

"Yes."

"Are you sure?"

Jolene nodded. "Yes. Here. I'll even give you my number if for some miraculous reason I do not show up on time." She swiped the pen from Ellie's hand and scribbled her number into the corner of her planner. She handed back the pen as she stood up. "Sorry, what's your name again?"

"Ellie Gallagher."

Jolene put on her aviators. "Right. Okay. I'm Jolene. See you on Sunday at eight p.m. in the library, Ellie!"

Ellie chuckled. "At least you got my name right!"

CHAPTER FOUR

A smoothie or a milkshake?

Jolene glanced at the menu options again. She still had ten minutes before she was supposed to meet Ellie to discuss their project. A milkshake sounded appetizing at the moment, but Acapellago members weren't supposed to drink dairy products before singing and they had a rehearsal later in the evening. She didn't really believe in that mumbo jumbo, but just in case a group member walked in, she opted for a smoothie.

She paid for her freshly blended fruits and sat down in one of the booths near the back of the café to scroll through the news on her phone. Jolene's best friends often complained about her being glued to her phone. She was of the opinion that they just didn't understand that she already had one foot out in the real world. Her free time was spent listening to current events and checking her email for replies to the many job applications she had sent out. Mo and Natalie, on the other hand, still had plenty of time to enjoy their senior year and ignore the unknown future. Jolene knew she was meant to work in politics, but she was in a sort of limbo until she found an employer who agreed with her. Satisfied that all was well in the world—or as well as it could be nowadays—her thoughts turned to the midterm project that counted for forty percent of her final grade. Mehra was a stickler for good work. Jolene had taken a class with her as a junior and it had been near torture. It was the first time she had really needed to work in a class, but the lessons she had learned there had stuck with her, although not much of the material covered in 'SWaG 217: History of Queer Cinema' applied to her politically focused major. Luckily for her, Mehra was teaching Women in Politics this semester. It was her last degree requirement, and the reason she was able to graduate a semester early.

While she waited, Jolene noticed the packed café. The colder weather drove students inside for their study sessions, and approaching midterms meant that students took more study breaks as an excuse to get away from their textbooks and unwritten term papers. She saw a few couples spread out across the café. She rolled her eyes at the clear PDA that most of them exhibited, although she envied them. Still, if she had a girlfriend, she certainly wouldn't parade her around at the café. That train of thought dredged up memories of her last relationship, which had ended nearly two years ago.

The relationship had been doomed from the start. Jessica was a year older than Jolene and, at the time, they lived on the same floor in Buchman Hall. They hooked up at a Halloween party in the dorm and it had turned into an emotional whirlwind for both of them. Jolene still remembered that warm October night when she had dressed up as Wonder Woman at the request of her friends. They said she had the perfect body for it and her long, dark hair and chocolate-brown eyes dressed up the cheap costume Mo had purchased for her online.

Jessica was, admittedly, a bit of a hipster and hadn't put any effort into her costume. At the last minute, she had thrown together a sad attempt at 'Static Cling' and Jolene recalled the near collision with her in the hallway just before the party got underway. She remembered Jessica in a black tank top and underwear as she ran down the hall to her best friend's room.

"Louise! Do you have any clean socks?" she had screamed.

Later that night, they had struck up a conversation in the dining hall when they were both in search of a water fountain. Jessica asked Jolene to save her a dance and, already smitten, she had waited patiently for the next hour until Jessica came back and asked her onto the floor. The dance grew heated and ended with some sloppy kissing before they moved things upstairs.

Jolene shook off the memories and glared at two girls swapping spit by the window. Dating Jessica had been a mistake and she didn't like to dwell on it.

"Hey Jolene."

Ellie stood at the table.

"Hi Ellie. Sit down." Jolene motioned to the other side of the booth and moved her feet to give Ellie room to squeeze in. Jolene couldn't place her, but for some reason Ellie looked very familiar. They had class together, but she felt like there was something else. She eyed her classmate as she took off a thin rain jacket and sat down with a thump. Ellie had short, auburn hair and a small pink barrette clipped next to her ear. She was dressed very nicely in form-fitting pants and a striped sweater right out of a Banana Republic window display. Most girls at Jones wore sweatpants with slouchy sweaters on the weekends since the largely female environment allowed students the novel option of devoting time to their schoolwork instead of their looks. Not having men around was one of Jolene's favorite things about Jones University. She never felt pressured to wear fancy clothes or makeup, as was often the case at the political offices where she interned during the summers. At school, she slept in longer most days because she could wear whatever she wanted. Clearly, Ellie didn't feel the same way. A hint of makeup accentuated her shocking blue eyes and a deep color emphasized her Cupid's bow lips. Jolene's gaze settled on a small gold necklace resting at Ellie's throat. She quickly looked down at her own black T-shirt and jeans and shrugged. At least she was comfortable.

"So," Ellie began.

"So," Jolene replied.

Ellie glanced at the clock. "You were on time."

"Early, in fact. So I rewarded myself with a smoothie," Jolene said as she picked up her cup.

Ellie took a notebook out of her bag and dropped a pen onto the table. "Did you look over the requirements for the project?"

Jolene was amused at how obsessed this girl seemed to be with her assignments. Did she have any hobbies beside homework?

"I did," she answered. "Do you have any thoughts on the political system that you'd be interested in researching?" It would probably be better to let the bookworm pick the topic.

Ellie hesitated. "I'm not sure."

Jolene found that surprising. She would have expected her classmate to come prepared with three choices, along with documentation to support why they would be topics worthy of an A.

"Well, I have a few ideas."

"Please share," Ellie said. "I'm completely at a loss here. I honestly don't know much about foreign political systems and wouldn't even know where to begin the research about how women are represented worldwide. I only took this class because I like Hillary Clinton! I don't know how I'm going to write a ten-page paper on any topic. Thank god our presentations are only fifteen minutes long." Ellie clearly seemed frustrated.

Jolene, at least, was having fun. "Well, I guess it's good you have me for a partner. Don't worry so much. We'll be writing the paper together and I'm great at presentations. As for topics, I don't know whether someone else is going to pick it, but I think women in Irish politics would be fascinating." Jolene wondered whether the subject already bored Ellie but, hilariously, she had already begun writing the idea down in her notebook. "The population of Ireland is an almost even split at forty-nine/fifty-one, but there has only been a one-percent increase in women's representation in the Irish Parliament in the last twenty years. And, Ireland is currently eighty-fifth out of one hundred ninety countries in terms of measuring female representation. They're consistently falling further down the chart too." Jolene paused.

"Wow."

"Yeah. Do you think that interests you?" she asked. She knew that the key to a good group project was having everyone excited about the topic.

"Uh. Definitely," Ellie said. "That sounds like a really good idea. And we could incorporate how the representation of women in politics is probably one of the reasons women's health issues aren't advancing there." She paused. "They *aren't* advancing there, right?"

Jolene nodded at Ellie's hasty conclusion.

"You are correct with that one. They are intertwined subjects. I think Mehra will eat it up," Jolene added.

Ellie exhaled. "Well, that was easy, I guess."

"Yep. And painless too," Jolene agreed.

"How do you know so much about Irish politics off the top of your head?"

"I don't know. I guess some stuff just sticks with you," Jolene answered. It was the truth. Her interest in world politics stemmed from her lifetime interest in all things political. Even as a kid she had spent her afternoons doing her homework with CSPAN in the background. Knowing about women in political spheres was a particular interest now, since she hoped to join their ranks soon.

"Did you make up those statistics to impress me?" Ellie asked with narrowed eyes.

Jolene wanted to laugh, but played it cool. "Is that all it takes to impress you?" she asked with a glint in her eyes. After a moment, Ellie broke out into a huge smile. Her only thought was that it was a good thing Ellie appreciated cheeky humor because it was the only type that Jolene had mastered.

"Pretty much," Ellie answered.

Jolene felt relieved that Ellie actually could put aside academics. "Well, I'll have to remember that, but no, I didn't make them up."

"All right then. Consider me impressed. Do you want to sketch out our thesis? I can type it up and bring it to class on Tuesday," she offered as she flipped to a blank page in her notebook. She was back to business.

"Sure," Jolene said, resigned to surrendering a sunny Saturday afternoon to work.

They spent the next twenty minutes crafting a thesis and outlining paragraphs, which Jolene had to admit, were all pretty damn interesting. It made her eager to go on. After they each gave it one final glance and tweaked the wording in the opening sentence, Ellie sat back and sighed into the silence between them.

Jolene continued to puzzle about where she might have met Ellie but drew a blank. "Where do I know you from?" she finally asked.

"What?" Ellie frowned.

"You look so familiar." Jolene hesitated. "Have we taken another class together?"

"I don't think so. I'm a Museum Studies major," Ellie answered.

Jolene persisted. "Did you ever live in Buchman?"

"No. I've always been in the Quad."

Jolene still had no idea where they might have met. "I just feel like we've met before."

"Well, I know you from all a cappella group events," Ellie murmured. Her eyes remained glued to her notebook.

"Are you in a group?" Jolene asked.

"Yeah. Treasurer of the Jones Tones."

Of course. Ellie was an a cappella singer. Acapellago and the other groups on campus performed at events together a few times every year. How could she forget Ellie? She was a staple in the Jones Tones, and had been for years.

"You have a solo in *Uptown Girl*!" she exclaimed.

Ellie's cheeks bloomed with color. "Yeah. That's me."

"Ah. That explains it. You're a soprano, right?"

Ellie's face turned serious. "Yeah, but I'm supposed to be beatboxing for our next concert."

"What? Why?" Jolene asked. It wasn't every day that a senior lead vocalist switched to percussion.

"One of our juniors went abroad and we need someone to take over her solos. No one else volunteered."

Jolene suspected that Ellie's tendency toward academic overachievement could get her into trouble at a cappella rehearsals too.

"Are you any good?" Jolene didn't really see Ellie as a natural beatboxer. The *Uptown Girl* solo proved that she was best suited to singing the melody.

"No. I'm shit at it."

Jolene found Ellie's self-assessment amusing. A cappella melodrama was a constant in her life at Jones. Something about a cappella attracted all the drama queens, but she secretly enjoyed watching from the sidelines as all hell broke loose every few weeks. Still, Jolene could tell Ellie was being honest about her skill level. She didn't seem the type to self-deprecate just to fish for compliments.

"Well, I'm decent at percussion. Maybe I can help you out with it while we're working on our project since we'll already be meeting up."

Ellie looked completely nonplussed. "Decent?"

"Yeah. At least, that's what I've been told."

"Are you kidding me?" Ellie demanded.

Jolene didn't know how to answer. "No?"

"Your beatboxing on *Toxic* was some of the best I've ever heard," she admitted as their eyes locked.

Jolene grinned. "Don't you know it's a mortal sin to admit another a cappella group is better than your own?"

"I did not say that. I merely confessed that you are better than 'decent.'" Ellie was smiling again. She was so cute.

"Ah. Well, in that case, I won't tell on you," Jolene joked.

"Thanks."

"Really, though. Next time we meet up I will totally give you some pointers. But you might have to commit another mortal sin."

Ellie looked wary. "And what sin would that be?"

"You'll have to tell a member of an opposing a cappella group what song you're singing at your next concert," she replied with the sternest look she could muster.

Ellie gasped in mock horror. "Never! You're trying to trick me into revealing all our secrets! I've made a blood pact to take them to the grave!"

Jolene laughed until her sides hurt. Ellie's humor was unexpected but felt like a breath of fresh air each time she allowed that overachiever mask to slip. Jolene pushed her hair out of her eyes. "All right. You got me! But I'll never give up trying. Acapellago won't be stopped until we rule over all the a cappella groups on campus."

Ellie scoffed in disbelief. "Yeah. That'll *never* happen."

"So, when is a good time for you to meet again?"

Ellie consulted her planner. "How about Tuesday? Do you guys practice that night?" she asked.

"Nope. We're on Mondays, Thursdays and Saturdays. So I'm free."

Ellie hovered over an empty spot in her schedule with a pencil. "Is the café okay again? My shift ends at eight."

"Sure. You work here?" she asked.

"Yeah!" Ellie answered happily.

Jolene hadn't put that together before. She had been wrong about Ellie. She had a hobby *and* a job. Maybe she wasn't as uptight as she seemed after all.

"Cool." Jolene got up from the table and put on her sunglasses. "So, I'll see you then."

"Sounds great. Tuesday at eight. Right here."

"Yep. Wednesday at four in the library."

"Is this going to become a thing?" Ellie asked playfully.

"Maybe." Jolene winked.

CHAPTER FIVE

I don't think I can stand this.

"Well, don't look at *me*."

Ellie watched the drama unfold in front of the Jones Tones. Sylvia, the group's president, and Alyssa, Sylvia's on-again, off-again girlfriend, were fighting again. Ellie closed her eyes, wondering why they always seemed to save their heated discussions for an audience. The group didn't have time for this. They needed to practice their new parts, Ellie most of all, if they wanted to be ready for the upcoming jam. She still hadn't managed to figure out the beatbox, and each rehearsal seemed to devolve into a tiff of some kind. Meetings like this made Ellie anxious for college to be over. She hoped the workforce had less drama than the insular world of a cappella.

"I *am* looking at you," Alyssa snarled.

"Honey, this is not my fault," Sylvia argued. Her perfectly painted nails clawed tightly at her leggings as if she wanted to tear them to shreds in anger.

"Don't you dare call me 'honey' right now."

"Oh, don't pretend you don't love it."

"I'd love it a little more if you weren't being such a dick about this," Alyssa snapped.

Ellie and Gabrielle commiserated by means of a glance that said, "Oh, brother, not *this* again." Gabrielle, a junior, was definitely on Ellie's short list of candidates for president once she and the other seniors graduated. She would certainly do a better job than Sylvia. Ellie had no idea why last year's seniors had picked her for the task. She was self-absorbed, unreliable, and competitive. In reality, the only thing she brought to the group was a huge number of devotees who loved her sex appeal and flair for the dramatic. Unfortunately, the group was tired of her drama, and had been since week one.

When Gabrielle nodded toward the clock on the back wall, Ellie got the message. This had gone on long enough.

"Guys. Maybe we should put your conversation on hold for the moment. We only have this space reserved for another twenty minutes. Let's use our time wisely," Ellie suggested, hoping that the two drama queens would let it go for the good of the group.

Alyssa crossed her arms and breathed out harshly. She stared at the other group members, and then relented. "Fine. But this isn't over."

Sylvia just shook her head sullenly. Ellie exhaled, grateful that a momentary truce had been achieved. She decided to take charge, unwilling to let this group go off the rails—at best, a lousy legacy for her class.

"Okay. Let's all stand up and try the new one. First time with the lyrics sheets and then we're going to do it from memory. Sound good?" she asked.

Ellie's suggestion was met with eager nods as younger members positioned themselves in the usual semicircle. Fortunately for the group, Alyssa and Sylvia were placed in different sections for this particular song. Ellie wasn't sure they could make it through the number if they shared the same air. She took her spot on the end of the lineup while their newest member assumed her place as pitch. Ellie gulped as the song began and cleared her thoughts as she counted them in to start singing with her.

The group was doing pretty well, but Ellie felt that her beat was sluggish. Her beatboxing skills were no match for Tonya, who was abroad in India for the year. She tried to remember everything she could about beatboxing patterns, but no matter what she tried, it wasn't quite right and she felt herself more and more breathless with each chorus. As the song concluded, Ellie felt a blush up the back of her neck. She knew the group heard her mistakes. With percussion, there was no place to hide. Ellie felt exposed, unsure if she would ever be able to master this talent.

"Ellie, I think you were off a little bit," Gabrielle said quietly.

"Yeah, I know. I'm going to practice it, guys. I promise."

"You'll get it," Sylvia added, determination in her voice.

Ellie was taken aback. It wasn't very often that Sylvia acted like a real leader. Today wasn't one of those days, as evidenced from her earlier squabble with Alyssa. Still, her ability to inspire confidence was a bonus that Ellie hadn't expected. It helped when somebody believed she could do it, even if that person was Sylvia.

"Should we try it again?" Gabrielle asked.

Ellie nodded. "Yeah. Let's give it a go."

She watched the other Jones Tones drop their lyric sheets to the ground. Maybe they could pull this performance together after all. They still had two weeks before their jam in front of an audience. Ellie wondered whether Jolene's proposal to help her with beatboxing had been serious. She hoped so, but feared that the offer had been more casual than real.

Her thoughts about the question dissipated as the pitch counted them in for another attempt at the song. She centered her thoughts only on the beat and surrendered to the tempo.

CHAPTER SIX

This seems kind of childish.

Jolene couldn't believe she was actually coloring. With crayons. She looked down at the mostly blank page under her fingers before selecting a purple crayon for the butterfly in the top corner of the image.

"I can't believe you talked me into this," she admitted.

"Think of it as a study break," Mo replied, digging through the box to locate a specific yellow crayon.

"Seems kind of childish," Natalie added from the couch behind them.

"That's what I was just thinking!" Jolene exclaimed.

They had been hunched over the coffee table for a few minutes, but Jolene was still hung up on the fact that they were coloring like preschool children. It seemed to Jolene that a Saturday night in a college town might be better spent on something other than the secret personal supply of coloring books, crayons and scented markers of one of her best friends.

"Channeling your inner child is good for the soul. That's why Natalie isn't coloring. She doesn't have a soul," Mo joked.

Natalie, typing on the laptop perched on her belly, stuck her tongue out at the two of them.

"How's Ian?" Jolene asked. She figured that Natalie was probably chatting with her long-distance boyfriend.

"He's good. Busy. I think he's going to come visit in two weeks."

"Over his fall break?" Mo asked.

"Yeah."

"Do you miss him?" Mo practically cooed.

"No. We soulless individuals don't have that capability," Natalie retorted with good-natured sarcasm.

The trio laughed, and Jolene relaxed. Schoolwork was an ever-present specter in her life, but she really enjoyed this quiet time with her two best friends. Most of the girls that lived in Buchman Hall would be busy with homework or some type of social engagement on a Saturday. There were countless parties across campus and lots of events in their little college town but, for Jolene, nothing could beat just hanging out with people she liked.

"I wish we had some wine," Jolene sighed. "That would be like icing on the cake."

"I have some pinot upstairs," Natalie offered.

"Nose goes!" Mo yelled.

Jolene quickly smacked her finger to her face, not wanting to get up from the floor to retrieve the bottle. Natalie watched, an eyebrow inching toward her hairline.

Natalie sighed. "You guys know it's not that far away, right?"

Mo picked up another crayon. "Four flights up is three flights too many for me," she announced. "Plus, we're otherwise occupied being artistic over here."

"Fine," Natalie huffed. "I guess that's what I get for offering free booze." She levered herself off the couch, dramatically moaning and groaning for all she was worth. Jolene chuckled and returned her attention to her picture. The garden scene was coming together.

"What color should this flower be?" she asked. Mo was nearly done coloring an image of "Veterinarian Barbara," an off-brand Barbie that looked slightly deranged. It took her a second to realize that Mo had turned it into a "Vegetarian Barbara" by adding a plate of tofu in one of Barbara's hands and a PETA sign in the other.

"Pink, probably."

"You're probably right."

"I'm *always* right," Mo teased. She added some finishing touches to her work. Jolene picked up the pink crayon, remembering the perfectly placed barrette in Ellie's short auburn hair.

"So, I think I made a new friend," Jolene mentioned as casually as possible.

"Really? Who?"

"This girl in my SWaG class," she said. "We're paired up for a project. I think that we'll work well together. She seems like a handful, but I think you'd like her. She's obsessed with homework, just like you."

"Hey now!" Mo sputtered.

"I only speak the truth," Jolene continued sagely.

Mo narrowed her eyes. "Does that mean you think I'm a handful?"

Jolene shrugged. "If the shoe fits—"

"Oh, I see! Making fun of my tiny feet. I'll have you know that I'm no more of a handful than you. I just happen to come in a smaller package," Mo replied, throwing her bushy hair back over her shoulder proudly.

"Bite-sized?" Jolene asked.

"You *know* it!" Mo's shark-like grin widened.

"Did I hear someone say candy?"

Natalie strode into the room, wine bottle clutched against her chest and three sippy cups hooked between her fingers.

"No. Jo's just tormenting me for being tiny," Mo said, leaping up from the floor to intercept the wine.

"No. I was tormenting her for being a handful," Jolene corrected.

Natalie handed Jolene a cup. "Well, we all know *that's* the truth."

"Can't we have *anything* age-appropriate tonight?" Jolene moaned as her friends poured the wine.

"Excuse you," Natalie said. "I think that Dora the Explorer is extremely age-appropriate. Ages five and up, dude! Also, you're coloring right now, so you're not allowed to judge my dishware."

Jolene sighed and sipped.

"Wine is age-appropriate," Mo added.

"My boyfriend is age-appropriate," Natalie continued, her eyebrows wiggling meaningfully.

Mo covered her ears and pressed her face against the coffee table. "Ew. No. I really do not want to hear it."

"Well, it's not my fault that I'm the only one with sexy stories to tell. Maybe if you two went out to one of the Quad parties tonight, we wouldn't have to talk about Ian being such a stud all the time."

"Stud!" Jolene joked. "I've never seen a stud with so many bow ties."

"Oh, please. Ellen DeGeneres has lots of bow ties," Natalie retorted.

"Are you admitting Queen Ellen is a stud?" Jolene asked.

"I'm secure enough in my heterosexuality to admit that Ms. DeGeneres is, in fact, a stud."

Jolene was satisfied. "I'm so proud of you."

"Is she done yet?" Mo whined, still crumpled onto the coffee table.

"Yes," Jolene patted her friend on the back, "You're safe. We're talking about lesbians again."

"Thank goodness. I'm trying to unleash my childish side tonight. I don't need references to all that straight mumbo jumbo right now," she said, waving her arms in Natalie's direction.

"I like to make you squirm," Natalie smirked.

Jolene coughed under her breath. "That's what he said."

"Oh, come on!" Mo pleaded. "Jo, you have to promise me that the moment you start dating someone, you will overshare everything about it. I need to start living vicariously through someone who isn't straight."

"I don't think I can make any promises," Jolene replied. "I don't see any romantic prospects in my future."

"What about that group project girl?" Mo asked. Natalie's gaze was particularly unrelenting.

"Who?" Jolene asked innocently.

"You said she was like me, so she must be cute," Mo teased.

Jolene shook her head. "I barely know her."

"You will after working on a project together!" Mo pointed at Jolene with a crayon.

"I don't think she's gay. She's pretty femme. I mean, she wears skirts. Barrettes in her hair and all that," Jolene explained.

"That doesn't mean anything," Mo responded. "She goes to Jones, after all."

"Hey!" Natalie interjected.

Mo held up her hands in defense. "All I'm saying is that there are a lot of queer and questioning girls here. I'm not saying we're all gay. Particularly you, Miss Natalie. You're as straight as the Prime Meridian."

The three friends burst into laughter that, to their delight, disturbed the quiet autumn evening. Once the giggles subsided, Jolene took another mouthful of wine.

"Just promise that you'll tell me if anything transpires. Otherwise, I'm going to have to binge *The L Word* again and we all know how that turns out every time."

"Oh, please no," Natalie moaned.

"My thoughts exactly." Mo nodded.

CHAPTER SEVEN

Are you serious? Right now?

From behind the register, Ellie watched a first-year student ponder the large menu board overhead. She had been standing there for at least three minutes. Ellie checked the clock on the back wall; it was 8:02. She scanned the booths and doorway, looking for Jolene. They were scheduled to meet at eight, and she was now officially late but this one time, it might be okay if Jolene didn't show up on time. Ellie glanced at the girl in front of her and cleared her throat.

After another full minute of uncertainty, the girl decided on an Oreo milkshake. Ellie completed the transaction and put the milkshake together as quickly as possible. It was more complicated than the far more popular latte or caramel macchiato that she had hoped the girl would pick. Realizing that it was 8:07 when she handed the shake to the customer, she tore off her apron and walked into the back room. Rose was at her small desk, surrounded by time sheets and work schedules for the weekend.

"Hey, my last customer just reminded me that I owe you some Oreos. I promise I'll bring them on Friday," Ellie said as she clocked out.

"All right. I'm holding you to that. No paycheck until I get my bribe," Rose joked.

With a quick farewell, Ellie slipped back out into the café and looked for the familiar beanie and long black hair. She walked to the very end of the room, about to give up, when she saw Jolene, stretched out in the last booth with her earphones in and eyes closed. Ellie pinched the toe of Jolene's scuffed leather boot.

Jolene opened her eyes and pulled out her earphones. "Hey!"

"Sorry for making you wait," Ellie apologized.

"Not a problem," Jolene responded. Ellie was grateful Jolene was so easygoing about tardiness.

"So, did you want to work here or should we find somewhere else?" Ellie felt nervous but couldn't figure out exactly why. It could be the looming project, which represented a huge percentage of their final grade. Maybe it was Jolene's offer to help her with beatboxing. She still wondered whether Jolene had been joking about the offer to help, but decided not to bring it up just yet. They needed to stay focused on the project at hand.

"I think here is pretty good. It's quiet and the booths are comfy." Jolene nodded as she sat up.

Ellie liked Jolene's easygoing attitude. She sank down across from her partner and let out a sigh. "Ah. It feels good to get off my feet."

"Long shift?" Jolene asked.

"Yeah. Some days it's really rough," Ellie answered, but if she was being entirely honest, almost every day was rough for her. She looked forward to Thanksgiving break, but knew that she had a lot to get done before then.

"I feel you there." Jolene's response shook Ellie from thoughts of upcoming schoolwork.

Ellie smiled at her, but quickly looked away once their eyes met.

"So, Professor Mehra approved the topic." In class earlier that day, Ellie had been able to sit in her usual seat by arriving five minutes early, happy that the intruding sophomore was forced to find a different seat. The girl still had a lot to learn about class etiquette. But her happiness slipped away when, a few minutes later, Jolene, absorbed in her music, walked past her to the last row of seats again. She hadn't even looked at Ellie. Truth be told, she had hoped that Jolene would sit next to her. Professor Mehra had collected their thesis submissions at the beginning of class and returned them while they discussed another reading in smaller groups. Everyone in her group had read the article this time, but the conversation never reached the depth that she had experienced in her discussion with Jolene. They just kept circling around the same argument, obviously all in disagreement but unable to find anything to back up their feelings. Ellie brushed thoughts of the disappointing discussion away as she took their thesis out of her bag. At the top of the paper, in blue Sharpie, was Mehra's comment: *Wonderful topic! Can't wait for more!*

"That looks like a good sign," Jolene said as she reached across the table for the paper. She flipped it around to read over their work again.

"It is. So, let's start with the structure of our presentation." When Jolene took out her laptop to take notes, Ellie became distracted by all the stickers on its cover. NPR seemed to feature most prominently, but others caught her attention. She recognized one for a local band that a lot of Jones students loved, and another bore a quote from the movie *Pitch Perfect*, an instant classic within a cappella circles. She frowned at the few she didn't recognize, including a spaceship of some kind and a tiny map she had never seen before. She made a mental note to look them up later.

Ellie refocused on the discussion, happy to add her own suggestions. As she spoke, Jolene typed and then turned the laptop to show Ellie a few articles she found to support both of their ideas. Ellie's attention moved to the page of notes on the other side of the screen. Jolene used little stars every so often when she was particularly happy about a certain point. Ellie found that to be really endearing, albeit a little juvenile. She was amused anyway.

They were most divided on the issue of where to include a discussion of Ireland's abortion laws, but decided to touch on it in the paper rather than during the presentation. Together, they found three scholarly articles that looked promising and a few newspaper articles that had a definitive stance on their topic.

Ellie thought back to other group projects she'd experienced at Jones and couldn't think of another time when she had faced so little trouble with a partner. Most times, collaboration with someone unfamiliar seemed to be an uphill battle, but Ellie felt at ease when talking politics with Jolene. It just came naturally. In fact, she found herself looking at Jolene a little too much, but she was highly impressed by the girl sitting across from her. Jolene had a habit of citing political polls from various cities and states in America to support her statements, and a knack for answering almost any political process question that Ellie could come up with. She actually caught herself trying to think of more questions, just to hear Jolene's answers and see the spark that came into her eyes when she launched into an argument. Ellie knew she could now put a name to the nerves she had been feeling earlier in the night when she first sat down at the booth. She had a crush.

Jolene interrupted Ellie's thoughts. "It's getting kind of late," she said.

A look at the clock confirmed Jolene's comment. Ellie closed her notebook. "Yeah. Should we call it a night?"

"At least the homework part," Jolene said. "Are you chickening out of the beatboxing tutorial that I promised you?"

"I kind of thought you were joking about that," Ellie admitted.

"No way. I never joke about a cappella," Jolene answered warmly. "I can impart all my wisdom while walking, if that helps."

Ellie thought that walking was probably a good idea. If Rose saw her beatboxing in the corner of the café, she'd probably spend an entire shift pestering Ellie about it. "Okay. You live in Buchman, right?"

"I do," Jolene answered as she packed up her laptop.

"It's on my way home."

"Great. Let's head out."

They grabbed their bags and jackets. Jolene held the door for Ellie, who shoved her hands into her too-small coat pockets once outside. The New England winter would soon be upon them.

While they strolled toward the center of campus, Ellie listened intently to Jolene's enthusiastic advice about beatboxing.

"It's also important to remember that half of the noise you're trying to make comes from the inhale," Jolene continued. "Do you find yourself getting breathless?"

"Yeah," Ellie answered. But her mind supplied another part to that answer. *Only when I'm around you.* She felt the blush rise to her cheeks, despite the chill in the air.

"That means you're not using the inhale enough. The best advice I could give you would be to practice a simpler pattern and work on that until you master the breathing. Repeat circular patterns." Jolene chatted on. Ellie felt like she should be taking notes, especially because part of her brain was zeroing in more on Jolene's mouth than the noises that were coming out of it. Still, she joined in on a few of Jolene's percussion tutorials, trying to match her own rhythm to the other girl's. She could feel the difference when she followed Jolene's advice, but she was startled out of her reverie when her partner stopped suddenly.

Ellie broke off a particularly good pattern, noting that Jolene seemed a little self-conscious. "What?"

"Um. We're here."

Ellie was surprised to realize that they stood outside Buchman. She hadn't even noticed how far they walked and couldn't remember crossing at the traffic light.

Jolene dragged a boot across a crack in the pavement. "Yeah. Well, I hope that helped. I could send you the links to some tutorial videos that I've used before, if you want."

"That would be great, thanks," Ellie said, looking down bashfully.

"Well, thanks for walking me home." Jolene already had her keycard in her hand, her mouth quirked up. Her crush wouldn't go away if Jolene kept saying vaguely flirtatious things like that. She swallowed down her nerves and tried to act cool.

"It was my pleasure. It's a cappella law that you have to be chivalrous to anyone teaching you the proper way to do vocal percussion," Ellie said happily. "Thanks again for the advice."

"Anytime. See you in class?"

Ellie didn't want to blush in front of Jolene for a second time in one evening. "Yes," she answered quickly.

"Okay," Jolene turned and bounded up the three steps to the front door. "Oh, I meant to ask. What song are you doing beats for, anyway?"

"*Can't Take My Eyes Off of You* by The Four Seasons." Ellie shook her head as she blinked away, acutely aware of the irony.

"Hm. That's a classic. I can't wait to hear it."

Ellie watched as Jolene retreated into the warmth of Buchman Hall and pinched the bridge of her nose. Ellie had no idea what was going on. She was losing control of her emotions. If she didn't tread carefully, her little crush could develop into something more. Jolene was her project partner and the project had to come first. The whole point of going to class was to get the grade, not a girlfriend. Maybe after the semester was over and they weren't in class together she might try to make a move, but now was not the time. Ellie continued her slow walk back to the Quad and reminded herself that she was too busy for a girlfriend.

CHAPTER EIGHT

Ellie is adorable.

Jolene took the steps two at a time until she reached her floor. Inside her room, she toed off her boots and closed the blinds. Wednesday was the one day every week that she got a chance to sleep in, and she refused to allow the sunlight to dictate what time she got up.

Jolene thought back to her meeting with Ellie. She was, maybe, the most motivated person Jolene had ever met. She would at least give Mo a run for her money. Ellie was already deeply invested in the project, volunteering to organize the slides for the presentation and read an extra scholarly article to support their final argument. Jolene certainly had more of an understanding of the political system, but Ellie stole the show when it came to class participation. They complemented each other perfectly for this assignment. Usually group projects were tedious and at least half thrown together at the last minute but Jolene didn't see that happening this time.

She strode across the hall to wash her face, all the while thinking more about how odd it must have looked to a passerby to see two girls beatboxing back and forth at each other in the middle of campus, especially at such a late hour. Oh well. Anything for a cappella.

Jolene put on her pajamas and climbed into bed with her laptop. She was almost done checking CNN when her phone buzzed on the desk. She growled and threw back the covers. She didn't recognize the number but opened the message out of curiosity.

Hey. It's Ellie. Thanks again for the help tonight.

Jolene thought back to the moment in class when she had scribbled her number in Ellie's planner. This was turning out to be fun. Jolene wished that they had met years earlier, confident that they would have become best friends. Or maybe something more. That thought stuck in her head since her conversation with Mo and Natalie. If only she wasn't graduating after this semester, perhaps it could've been something. But such a daydream was foolish. She heard her grandmother's voice reminding her that work should come first. Always. She burrowed back under the covers and typed out her reply.

Anytime. :)

Jolene was just about to put the phone down when an overjoyed emoji greeted her in reply. She chuckled for a moment but then reminded herself that she had just promised herself that this wouldn't happen. There was no avoiding her future beyond Jones University. She had to figure it out, since it would come sooner than for most of her friends; it wouldn't be long until she would be a college graduate and a full-fledged adult in the real world. She needed a job and an apartment, and hadn't even decided where she'd live. She felt burned out by the mess of unanswered questions in her brain and let NPR soothe her as she drifted off to sleep. She'd get the project done, she resolved, and move on like the adult she was supposed to be.

CHAPTER NINE

Don't forget to breathe, dummy.

Ellie made herself gulp in some air as she walked into the classroom. Nerves about her upcoming presentation had caused her stomach to churn all morning. Like it or not, today would be the day forty percent of her grade was decided. She quickly spotted Jolene, who had stolen her usual seat in the second row. She was glad for something to take her mind off the looming prospect of public speaking. Ellie climbed the few stairs to her row and settled down in the open seat next to Jolene. They had spent the last three nights working on the final touches of their presentation and paper. Ellie was pleased with the result, but still felt fidgety. She still didn't understand why she could sing in front of hundreds of people without a second thought while public speaking reduced her to a shivering mess. As a typical overachiever, she stressed whenever a grade hung in the balance but, in this case, felt confident that if anything went awry, Jolene was there to help. Over the past week, Ellie had realized how well they worked together. The project was definitely worth an A but she was even more pleased to have finally enjoyed contributing to a group project. She and Jolene made an amazing team, one that Ellie doubted she would ever be able to replicate. Her only regret was that almost all their time together had been devoted to the project. She zoned out, wishing that their passionate conversations had been about their lives and hopes and future plans rather than Ireland's political structure. She would have gladly exchanged their many conversations about the Taoiseach and the few women representatives in the Oireachtas for a simple discussion about Jolene's favorite film or what she thought about participating in No Shave November. Ellie glanced at Jolene, who seemed totally at ease, leaning back in her desk chair and rummaging through her shoulder bag.

Ellie noticed the anticipatory bounce in her own left knee. "Are you ready?" she asked.

Jolene looked up enthusiastically. "Yeah. Are you?"

Ellie let out a deep breath. "I guess."

"Don't worry so much."

Ellie only shook her head. Easier said than done. She settled back into her seat and waited as other students went to the front of the lecture hall to give their presentations but she was distracted by thoughts of her own. About halfway through class Jolene leaned over and whispered into Ellie's ear.

"Our presentation is going to kick ass."

Ellie beamed, but felt a blush threatening to creep up from under the collar of her dress shirt, which she had ironed just for their presentation. Jolene wasn't helping the nerves she had been fighting off since she stepped into the room. She only replaced the nervous-student butterflies with nervous-crush butterflies. At that moment, it was hard to say whether she was more concerned about Professor Mehra's assessment of her, or Jolene's.

Sooner than Ellie would have liked, it was their turn to present. Together, they made their way up to the front of the room and opened the PowerPoint that Ellie had spent far too many hours finessing the night before. Jolene was in charge of presenting the introduction and first three slides, but before she got started, she glanced at Ellie with a final reassuring look. Ellie tried to channel Jolene's serene attitude and nodded in reply as her partner launched into their introduction. Jolene's words washed over Ellie. Her black braid swung loosely against her shoulders as she spoke animatedly about the Irish government. Ellie felt calm for the first time all day. Something about Jolene's demeanor helped her to realize that no matter what, they would do fine on this assignment. Jolene had been right—their presentation would kick ass. With that thought in mind, she took over on the fourth slide with a confidence that she had never experienced.

Fifteen minutes later, their classmates clapped politely as Professor Mehra nodded enthusiastically. As they returned to their seats, she caught Ellie's attention.

"I can't wait to read the full report," her professor confided quietly.

Ellie felt even more proud of their work. She followed Jolene back to their seats and practically collapsed onto the chair and closed her eyes to collect her wits. Suddenly, the ghost of fingertips brushed over the back of her hand. When her eyes snapped open, Jolene's gaze was fixed on her.

"We did it."

Ellie's heart still felt stuck in her throat. "Yeah, we did."

They looked at one another for a few interminable seconds before they were shaken out of their reverie by the next group presentation. Ellie's heartbeat continued beating a too-loud thump in her ears as she realized Jolene wasn't going to move her hand. She held her breath, considering what to do, when Jolene's thumb rubbed a small circle over the knuckle of Ellie's pinkie. She exhaled, knowing in that moment that she was a goner; she was hooked on Jolene.

Ellie didn't hear her classmates talking anymore. Her whole world had shrunk down to hands on the desktop and the unbelievable person seated to her left. She slowly rotated her wrist, so that their fingers were loosely interlaced, her attention focused solely on their hands. She feared that looking elsewhere would destroy the moment.

The rest of the class slipped by quickly and Professor Mehra dismissed class with congratulations to each group. Jolene squeezed her hand once, and then disentangled their fingers.

Jolene stood up. "I have to go," she said as she gathered her bag.

Ellie was at a loss for words. Were they going to discuss the hand-holding that had lasted nearly twenty minutes? She wanted to know what it meant, but stifled the many questions that percolated in her mind.

Instead, she nodded. "I guess I'll see you later then."

"Yeah," Jolene replied. She slipped on her earphones and beanie, and headed for the door.

Ellie watched her go, and wondered whether she had just missed an important opportunity to change something between them.

CHAPTER TEN

What is wrong with me?

Jolene sat in the dining hall at her usual table across from Mo and Natalie, but felt disinterested in their discussion about the finer points of menstrual cups. Instead, she thought about Ellie. Jolene's heart had been racing since the presentation. Ellie had aced her sections, and Jolene recalled her adrenaline rush after it was over. She liked Ellie a lot—maybe *more* than a lot. On several occasions, she caught herself staring into those bright blue eyes for a little longer than the situation demanded.

And yet, Jolene had the uncomfortable sense that Ellie misinterpreted the touch of her hand after the presentation. It had been a simple gesture, as far as she was concerned, but when Ellie intertwined their fingers, it seemed that she had perceived something other than assurance—a thought that terrified Jolene. She was graduating in two months, and couldn't afford to get bogged down in a silly crush.

"Jolene!"

"What?" Startled, Jolene looked up from her food.

"What's up with you?" Natalie demanded with a frown.

Jolene found her friends' scrutiny embarrassing. She took a bite of mashed potatoes to buy some time, in the hopes that the conversation might veer in another direction, but no luck.

"Nothing. I'm just thinking some things through," she stammered.

"Anything we can help with?" Mo offered.

Jolene considered the offer and decided that if anyone could help her with this situation, it was these two women.

"Well, remember when I told you about that girl I was doing the group project with?" Mo and Natalie nodded in unison. "Well, I think I might have done something really stupid."

Mo's eyes widened. "Oh god! What did you do? Please tell me you didn't fail the project."

Jolene couldn't help her amusement. Mo was perpetually preoccupied with good grades—something that she and Ellie would find in common if they ever met.

"No. I might have hit on her and instigated some awkward hand-holding during class."

Natalie and Mo looked dumbfounded.

"And?" Natalie finally asked with a perplexed look.

"And, I'm graduating so soon that it's only going to cause someone pain in the end. I don't want to hurt her. I want to leave college with a diploma, not a broken heart."

Her friends looked at one another with matching smirks.

"Listen, Jo, I know you want us to agree with you and tell you how dumb you are for having a crush, but that's not what real friends do," Natalie explained. "We're here to tell you that it's okay. In fact, it might be a good thing for you."

Mo nodded. "Yeah. I think it's great news."

"Well, that's all fine and dandy for you guys, but I don't have any idea what I'm doing! Shouldn't I be more concerned with other things in my last semester of college? Like applications and apartment hunting?"

"Do you like her?" Natalie asked flatly.

That was the big question, wasn't it? Yes, she liked Ellie. She knew deep down that they somehow fit together in a way she hadn't felt with anyone before. At the same time, what would be the point of diving into a relationship headlong when she knew from the start that it would have to end? She voiced these opinions and was quickly rebuffed by Mo.

"If it makes you happy and she feels the same, then it doesn't matter how long it lasts or if it's serious. You're both adults and you can do whatever the hell you want. There's always long distance once you graduate. Or, you could end up staying close by! The point is that you don't know what will happen. Maybe she's not even interested."

"Ouch," Natalie said, looking at Mo with an arched eyebrow.

Mo shrugged. "Hey! It's a possibility. I'm just throwing it out there."

Ignoring Mo, Natalie glared at Jolene. "So, what are you going to do about it?" she asked.

"I have no clue," Jolene answered nervously.

"Maybe you could start by asking her out? Like normal people," Natalie offered. "Otherwise, you'll have to settle for Mo so I can finally use the amazing portmanteau MoJo to talk about you as a couple!"

They all giggled as Mo started bemoaning the fact that she had somehow become friends with an English major that used words like "portmanteau" in everyday conversation. As her friends exchanged loving barbs, Jolene decided that maybe it wouldn't be so bad to give it a try. She could at least find out whether Ellie was interested, although based on everything she knew, she couldn't imagine that Ellie would say no. Jolene excused herself from another night of hanging out in the living room to watch overly dramatic Shonda Rhimes programming and headed back upstairs to get some homework done. All her romantic worries melted away once she was settled into the desk chair with a blank document open waiting for her to begin a new assignment.

An hour later, the chime of her phone startled her. Ellie's name appeared on the screen.

Hey. I don't know if you're interested, but my group will be singing next Friday in the Student Lounge. Nine p.m. Hope to see you there.

Jolene took a deep breath, knowing how Mo and Natalie would tell her to take this opportunity to make a move. What did she really have to lose? She tapped out her reply and pushed send before she could rethink her decision.

It sounds great. I can't wait to hear your new beatboxing skills. But, I was kind of hoping we could do something sooner?

She waited for a response, staring blankly at the phone. Her pulse quickened when she saw the small bubble signaling that Ellie was typing a reply.

Like what? Miss doing homework with me already?

Jolene felt a warmth in her chest. Yes, she did miss the homework. But admitting that was a bit too much. She had a reputation to maintain, after all. And she knew that it wasn't the homework part of the equation that she would be missing now that the project was complete.

Milkshakes at the café? Tomorrow at eight?

The response seemed to take forever. Her knee knocked hurriedly against the desk as she waited. Finally, the bubble reappeared.

Sure! I'll see you there.

Excitedly, she typed another reply.

I'm looking forward to it.

Jolene waited for a further response, but nothing came. Eventually, she returned to her assignment but all she could think about was Ellie. A relationship could change her world, but only if she let it happen.

CHAPTER ELEVEN

She's going to love it.

Present in hand, Ellie rounded the corner and knocked lightly on the door. Rose was buried in paperwork but waved Ellie into the cramped office.

"Hey girl! Come on in!"

Ellie grinned. "I have a surprise for you," she said.

"If it's that bribe you owe me, then that does not count as a surprise," Rose quipped as she closed her laptop.

Ellie pulled the Golden Oreos out of her shoulder bag. "Okay. Well then, I have a bribe for you," she admitted, folding into the chair opposite the desk.

Rose bolted up to grab the package and tore it open. She sat on the edge of her desk and pulled out a handful of cookies.

"So, besides bringing me your generous gift, why are you here on your day off?" she asked as she threw an Oreo onto Ellie's lap.

"What, I can't just swing by to see your lovely face?" she replied, happy to have something to munch on while Rose began her inevitable interrogation.

Rose's eyes narrowed suspiciously. "No. That's not your style."

Ellie finished her cookie as she mustered up the courage to ask for the advice she sorely needed. Rose had been like a big sister to Ellie through all her years at Jones. Her frank advice and upbeat attitude were admirable qualities in a boss, but even better in a friend.

"Do you think it's weird to hold hands with someone you barely know?" she asked, picking at the corner of a purchase order sticking out from under her thigh.

Rose contemplatively licked the icing out of the middle of an Oreo. "I guess it depends on the person. Why do you ask?" she asked.

Ellie cleared her throat and looked down at her shoes, ready to admit what had been haunting her since her SWaG class on Tuesday.

"I held hands with a classmate yesterday after a presentation. For about twenty minutes." She winced.

"Was the presentation particularly romantic?" Rose asked, suddenly serious.

"No, it was about politics. In Ireland."

"Well, what could be more romantic than that? Tell me everything!" Rose demanded, hopping down to settle behind her desk.

"Her name is Jolene and we paired up for this project in my SWaG class. She's a senior American Studies Major and she's in Acapellago. She's beautiful and smart and, like, so driven despite having this cool-girl attitude all the time. And I really like her. After our presentation yesterday we went back to our seats and—it sounds so stupid—but she touched the back of my hand. I just lost it and held on for dear life for the rest of the class period. And then I invited her to come see my a cappella jam next week, since she helped me practice, but she responded by asking to meet me tonight for milkshakes."

"So, you're wondering if she asked you on a date after you sort of asked her on a date?" Rose asked as she picked up another Oreo.

"Yeah, I guess. I didn't mean it as a date, but—" Ellie had wanted to take the invitation back the moment she sent it. She was now terrified to look out into the audience and see that familiar smirk waiting there. She didn't want to be distracted by those sharp cheekbones or that black braid of hair that looked oh-so inviting to touch. The butterflies she had felt before the presentation in Professor Mehra's class were nothing compared to the ones she had now.

"Well, inviting her to your show was a good start," Rose said, launching into advice mode. "I don't see why you need my opinion. I think anyone who would hold your hand for that long must feel something. The milkshake thing is probably just a way to see you before the concert. A week is a long time to wait, especially when you're as young as the two of you. I think you worry too much."

"Rose, you know me. I worry constantly," Ellie confessed.

"Yes, you do and I fear I'll never break you of that habit. You'll give yourself an ulcer. Anyway, you'll sing your heart out at the concert, but in the meantime, you have another opportunity to show that girl you mean business. I wish I was here tonight. I would be watching you like a hawk the whole time," Rose said as she slid the cookies into her desk drawer. "Now, get going and go pick an outfit! Some of us have work to do."

Ellie set out for the Quad with a jumble of thoughts. Her first worry was for the upcoming performance. Her beatboxing debut would take place in only a week. As she walked across campus, that worry grew. She pictured all the possible mishaps that could happen at the jam. She could lose her voice dramatically at a pivotal moment, just like poor Carlotta in *The Phantom of the Opera*. Or she might see Jolene's look of approval disappear as the realization hit—the beatboxing lessons hadn't helped her at all. Uneasiness festered as she walked back into the Quad. She decided to spend the rest of the afternoon rewatching some of the tutorial videos Jolene had shared with her after their late-night lesson. The only thing she could control now was her performance. She wanted to impress Jolene, but more importantly, she wanted to make herself—and the Jones Tones—proud.

Her second worry was about her date with Jolene later that evening. Or not-date. She still wasn't sure. Either way, she wanted to look good. Her mind drifted as she watched the beatboxing tutorials. She thought about Jolene's long mane of hair draped over her shoulder, her chocolate-brown eyes and athletic body. Distracted, she closed the tab and took a long shower instead, hoping that the water would wash away her scattered thoughts.

CHAPTER TWELVE

Maybe this was a bad choice.

Jolene glanced through the windows of the café as she entered the Campus Center, her usual suave attitude overshadowed by doubt. Not only was she attempting to date someone in her last and most hectic semester of college, but she had also picked the worst possible spot for a first date. Ellie worked in the café. When the realization had hit as she walked across campus, her face flushed at the thought of her carelessness. Anything would have been better than the same milkshakes Ellie had to make for students all week long. She berated herself again, thinking it was a sign that this date was a very bad idea. She wondered if it was too late to play it off like two friends just hanging out.

"Probably," she said under her breath. The hand-holding incident screamed more than friends. She grabbed the door handle, determined not to let her own screwup ruin her chances.

"Hey Jolene!" she heard from over her shoulder. Ellie strode over from the small couches tucked in the corner outside the café's entrance. She looked stunning in a simple pearl-colored dress and a tweed blazer. Jolene swallowed. She was used to seeing Ellie dressed up for class, but this was at a different level. Her mind supplied "first date outfit" instantly. She felt her palms go sweaty at the possibility. It had been so long since she had wanted to impress someone because she had a crush. Most of the time she just aimed to prove that she was a force to be reckoned with, either in the classroom or on the stage. Her personal life had been pretty unremarkable for a long time.

"Hi," was the only word she could get out, despite her runaway thoughts.

Ellie surveyed Jolene's long frame. "You look great," she remarked.

Jolene glanced down at herself. Her dark jeans and black leather boots were nothing special since she wore them almost every day. However, she had spent a long time deciding on the rest of her outfit. Her bed was littered with discarded options that both Mo and Natalie had vetoed. Luckily, they had all agreed on this combination. She knew the blue denim shirt poking out from under the camel-colored sweater contrasted nicely with her dark hair and tanned skin. Still, it couldn't compare to Ellie's outfit.

"That's what I was going to say to you," she answered, at a loss for anything else to say. "I like the Converse." Ellie looked down at her own feet, rocking back on her heels to flex her toes.

"They're my old reliables," Ellie explained with a grin. "Should we go in?"

Jolene hesitated, before voicing her worries. "It occurred to me on the walk over that you might be sick of the café milkshakes by now. Do you want to go somewhere else instead?"

Ellie paused before answering. "Well, I do get sick of making them, but I think they're pretty great, actually. I wouldn't mind some chocolate."

"We could always go to a bar in town or something," Jolene offered.

"Nah. I can never hear people when I go to a bar. It's always way too loud for my taste."

Jolene opened the door for Ellie. "Yeah, especially that dance-y one on the corner of Dean Street."

"Ugh! Yes. I've been there a few times with some girls from my a cappella group and it's always a mess."

They meandered toward the menu board above the register. "Do you go there for karaoke?" Jolene asked.

"No. I've actually never done karaoke before."

"Really?"

Ellie nodded.

"It's something Acapellago does at the start of every semester as a bonding activity," she explained.

"I don't think the Jones Tones are really a bonding type of group nowadays," Ellie admitted.

"Sounds exciting. I want to hear all about that drama," Jolene joked.

Ellie groaned. "You know they're going to hunt me down if I keep telling you all our secrets. She gestured toward the board. "What are you thinking of getting?"

"I usually go for the vanilla. Simple is best."

"Allow me," Ellie said. The woman behind the counter stepped up to the register. "Hey Xiaoli. Could I get a chocolate shake, no whip, extra cherries for myself and a vanilla shake for my boring friend over here?"

Friend. With that one word ringing in her ears, she knew that it wasn't enough to satisfy her now. Jolene's crush on Ellie had consumed her thoughts over the past week and her uncertainty had transformed into something definite.

The café worker moved to the ice cream case.

"Boring?" Jolene asked with a raised eyebrow.

"We all think people who order vanilla are boring. It's part of our training. Isn't that right?" she asked the other girl.

The Chinese girl snorted as she scooped ice cream from the containers. "Yeah. Rose encourages the judgment stuff from day one. I like to think it passes the time."

"I always considered it a classic." Jolene shrugged. "Nothing beats the original recipe."

"I think milkshakes are gross," Xiaoli responded as she turned on the blenders. "Anything else for you two?"

"Nope, that's it for now," Ellie answered.

"Okay. I'll bring them over to you when I'm finished. Seven bucks even."

Ellie pulled money from her blazer pocket.

"Hey. I should pay!" Jolene said, trying to prevent Ellie from handing over the cash. She had been the one to ask Ellie on the date, after all.

"Yeah, but I get the café discount," Ellie responded with a wink, moving Jolene's hand aside.

Xiaoli handed the change over the counter with a grin. Jolene walked toward one of the booths they had used for one of their late-night meetings for the SWaG presentation. It brought back fond memories of Ellie being totally in her element amidst their hastily scribbled notes and library books.

"Thanks for paying," Jolene said.

"You're welcome. Consider it a thank you for a job well done on the presentation and all the a cappella help," Ellie answered, looking down at her fingers as they traced over a smudge on the table.

"I really enjoyed working with you on the project. And the beatboxing was really fun. I like passing on the talents of Acapellago to less fortunate a cappella groups on campus." She watched Ellie roll her eyes. "But honestly, I'd be willing to help out anytime."

"Thanks," Ellie answered. "I'm still worried about performing next week, but I think it's a lot better than it was before you helped me. Hopefully, the audience thinks it's good."

"I'm sure they'll love it. I know I will," she answered.

They both leaned back as Xiaoli delivered their milkshakes. "Don't tell anyone, but out of all the staff, I make the best milkshakes. Enjoy!" she announced.

"How would you know?" Ellie called after her. "You don't even drink them!"

"The tip jar!" Xiaoli yelled from around the corner.

When Ellie laughed, her blue eyes crinkled around the edges, causing warm desire to rush through Jolene. It was a look Jolene could get used to.

"She seems like fun to work with," Jolene started.

"She is. I think she'll make assistant manager next year. Rose loves her."

"Rose is your boss?" Jolene asked.

Ellie sipped her milkshake. Jolene followed Ellie's lips intently, wondering what they would feel like pressed against her own.

"Yeah. She's been the manager here for over a decade. She graduated from Jones and never left."

"Wow. I can't imagine staying here for that long," Jolene said.

"Yeah, I'm not sure she even likes it that much. She never really told me why she stayed," Ellie said with a shrug. "I think it's hard for her to talk about."

"So, you're not hoping to stick around East Westwick after graduation?" Jolene asked, aware that it was a leading question.

"No way. I'd love to get to Washington DC, but who knows at this point?"

"That makes sense. There've gotta be a ton of museum opportunities in Washington. That's my dream city too," she explained.

"Yeah. It seems like the obvious place for a political person to go."

"Maybe we'll both end up there," Jolene mused.

"Maybe," Ellie replied wistfully.

They sipped their milkshakes before rehashing their presentation in Mehra's class. They discussed their own opinions of how they had fared and giggled about another group that had misspelled "Cameroon" on every slide of their PowerPoint.

"So. The hand-holding thing—" Ellie broached cautiously.

Jolene's mouth dried out. Now that they were on the topic, she didn't really know what to say.

"Yeah. I'm sorry if that made you uncomfortable. It just sort of happened, I guess," Jolene replied, hoping it didn't sound too nonchalant. It had been totally unplanned, but once their hands had linked Jolene realized she was reluctant to let go. She wanted to hold onto Ellie. Working with Ellie on their project had brought them closer as friends, but she would be lying if she said that was all she desired.

"I wasn't uncomfortable. It was just unexpected."

"Okay." Jolene felt relieved. It was a first step. Ellie stared at her. She seemed to be searching for something, but although Jolene had no idea what it was, she hoped she would pass whatever test Ellie was conducting.

"I wouldn't mind if it happened again," Ellie said.

Ellie's candor caught Jolene off guard.

"Just not during class. I usually spend the whole period taking notes," Ellie continued.

"Understandably," Jolene agreed, her hopes soaring.

She reached out the hand that wasn't chilled by the half-finished milkshake, and let her fingers trace over Ellie's hand, noting differences between them. Ellie's pale skin was lighter than her own, dotted with freckles and softer to the touch. Jolene felt her own calluses, from weight training at the gym with Natalie earlier in the week, catch along the softness beneath her fingers. Like Jolene, Ellie kept her nails short, but actually maintained them. Ellie didn't wear any jewelry except the delicate Jones class ring on her right hand. Jolene found herself captivated by Ellie's fingers as they began to intertwine with her own.

"I found this very distracting in class," Ellie said under her breath.

"Yeah, I did too," Jolene murmured.

Their thumbs continued to brush back and forth. Jolene discerned a light in Ellie's eyes that hadn't been there before. This was completely different from the first time she had held Ellie's hand. In class, she had acted out of fear, adrenaline and, maybe, a little desperation. Now, they were taking this step together. Neither of them was surprised by the touch this time. Yet, Jolene could still feel her heart thumping nervously. She cleared her throat and tried to redirect the discussion to something other than the places where their skin sparked against each other.

"So, tell me more about your a cappella drama," she said, hoping her voice sounded steady and knowing it probably didn't.

Ellie launched into a complicated story of two seniors in the Jones Tones who continually fought in front of the group. Her storytelling made Jolene forget about the sensitive touch connecting them. Instead, she focused on Ellie's retelling of the partial comedy and partial tragedy that comprised the relationship between her fellow group members.

"Half the time, we don't even know why they fight," she explained with a shrug.

"It sounds like they like the excitement of it all," Jolene added.

"Oh, yeah. They love that bit. I think they're both starving for the attention. It just so happens that the group is the perfect audience for their shenanigans three times a week," Ellie said.

"Did you ever think about kicking them out of the group for misbehavior?"

"No. Sylvia is the president, after all. It's barely worth it now. We'll all be gone after graduation, anyway. I just hope the people left in charge next year don't think this is how an a cappella group is supposed to operate." Ellie sighed.

Jolene squeezed Ellie's fingers, thinking again about her early graduation. She would be leaving Acapellago behind at the end of the semester. Luckily, their group had solid leadership that wouldn't be disrupted by her departure. Jolene opened her mouth to explain her worries about leaving Acapellago behind, but nothing came out. She snapped her jaw shut. What would Ellie say about her being a January graduate?

"Well, I'm all out of milkshake," Ellie said, sipping at the dregs left in the glass.

Jolene decided that discussion could wait for another day. They were just having fun. It wasn't anything serious. At least not yet. She slipped her fingers loose from the grasp that had been linking them for most of their conversation, but instantly missed the pressure of Ellie's small fingers wrapped up in her own.

"I think I'm going to go home to try and get some homework done." Ellie sighed.

Jolene was charmed by Ellie's dedication. It didn't seem like she ever stopped working. Once one project ended, another assignment took its place. Jolene admired her work ethic, but she was a little disappointed that their night would end so quickly.

"Can I walk you home?" she asked.

"Sure. To the Quad we go!" Ellie exclaimed as she bounced up from her seat.

Jolene watched her drop off their empty glasses with the girl behind the register. They exchanged a few words and, slyly, Ellie tried to steal the tip jar. Xiaoli grabbed at the repurposed coffee can, chiding Ellie in a voice loud enough to make a few heads around the café turn to see what was causing the commotion. Ellie handed the tip jar back with a gleam in her eyes. Jolene realized she must look idiotic, standing in the center of the café with a goofy look plastered across her face, but she couldn't help her reaction. She felt excited about the possibility of dating Ellie, but still worried about what would happen if she let herself get involved. The semester was almost halfway over, but that still left half a semester to explore. Maybe it wouldn't be so bad to let her emotions take over, at least for a little while. Jolene tried to school her features back to normal as Ellie met her at the exit, her dress rippling against her shapely legs.

"Ready?" Jolene asked.

"Yes ma'am," Ellie replied with a smile, opening the door for Jolene.

CHAPTER THIRTEEN

Play it cool!

Ellie's heart felt like it was moving more than a mile a minute. She welcomed the cool air as she and Jolene stepped out of the Campus Center. The not-date definitely seemed like a date now. She flexed her fingers, remembering Jolene's cool touch across the table. They walked in companionable silence, but with each step Ellie wondered what would come next. She closed her eyes for a second, remembering how after expressing interest in more hand-holding, Jolene had done just that. They seemed to be on the same page. She wondered if she should reach for Jolene's hand, swinging gently beside her own. She was so unsure of what to do next. Memories of high school boyfriends and rejection loomed large as a reminder of how little experience she had. Would Jolene know? Would she care? It had taken her years to finally admit to herself that she was bisexual, yet that discovery hadn't changed the fact that her few dates since then failed to develop into anything serious. She had been on a couple first dates during her time at Jones, but she had never been asked on a second one. But, if this tentative first step with Jolene was anything to go by, they were already doing better than her other attempts. As she debated silently about her next move, she realized time was running out.

"I had fun tonight," she said.

"Me too."

The cool girl routine was no help at all! They passed under the archway and entered the Quad.

"I like when we don't do homework together."

"We should do it again sometime." Ellie cleared her throat, hoping it didn't sound too desperate.

"I'd love that," Jolene replied, a smile tugging at the corner of her perfect mouth.

The hesitation between them was awkward. For a few seconds, Ellie contemplated a kiss. Was it too soon? As her eyes moved again to trace Jolene's lips, she felt the desire to stretch up the few inches to touch them with her own but her nerves told her otherwise. The thought made her tremble, with equal measures of anticipation and apprehension.

"Goodnight Jolene," she murmured. The anxiety won out. She walked up the few steps to the front door and quickly swiped her keycard.

"Goodnight!" she heard from over her shoulder as the door closed behind her.

Ellie leaned against the heavy door, her thoughts frayed at the edges. This was clearly more than friendship. The hand-holding proved they had a deeper connection, but it had been a long time since a girl had looked at her with clear desire in her eyes. And she had never felt her own attraction truly returned. Jolene's chocolate-tinged eyes promised the possibility of those emotions. Ellie felt hope blooming from somewhere deep inside and wanted more than anything to reach out and grab it.

Still, had she missed the moment to prove her interest? Perhaps Jolene thought she was too scared to act on the feelings she so clearly harbored, or assumed that Ellie was too busy with homework and a cappella duties to entertain the idea of a relationship.

Ellie took a deep breath, unwilling to let the opportunity pass by. She opened the door and ran off the porch into the cool night air. Her gaze settled on a shadow on the far side of the Quad. In the darkness, she could just make out Jolene's tan sweater.

"Jolene!" she called, sprinting after the tall woman. She hoped the moment was salvageable. Jolene turned in surprise at the sound of her name. Ellie sank into the soggy grass as she cut across the lawn. A few feet from Jolene, she slowed to catch her breath and push her nerves away.

Ellie was breathless. "I forgot something," she said.

Jolene's eyebrow perked up, but before she could ask, Ellie kissed her. Jolene tasted like vanilla, with lips softer than Ellie had imagined. The kiss alone was enough to make her want more.

"How could you forget that?" Jolene teased.

Ellie grinned. "I have no idea. I must be losing my mind."

"It happens to the best of us," Jolene assured her.

"Sorry," she said, apologizing automatically.

"You don't have anything to be sorry about," Jolene answered. The other woman leaned in, reaching up to hold Ellie's chin with those dexterous fingers that had been laced with hers earlier in the evening. "Nothing at all," she continued. Jolene leaned in for another kiss. Ellie inhaled sharply, wanting to remember every detail of the moment. The hand on her chin moved to circle around her neck. She felt Jolene's tongue tangle with her own. The tremble of nervousness was now replaced with a steady hum of want and desire. Their late-night study sessions and fleeting glances had all been building to this moment. The kiss wasn't perfect since they still had so much to learn about one another, but she warmed at the thought that with some more practice, it could get there.

"GET IT, GIRLS!"

The shout, which startled the two women from their reverie, came from a window somewhere in the Quad. They pulled back, their only remaining contact the hand that Ellie rested on one of Jolene's slim hips. Surprise gave way to giggles, and Ellie let her fingers slip away to her side, immediately yearning for the feeling of that warm body underneath her fingers.

"So," Ellie muttered, rubbing at the back of her neck.

"So," Jolene said with a grin.

"I'll see you in class on Tuesday?"

"Yeah. I'll be there," Jolene answered smoothly.

Jolene walked toward the archway leading to the rest of campus while Ellie basked in the knowledge that she had seized the moment and made it her own.

CHAPTER FOURTEEN

Jeez, the place is packed.

Jolene scanned the cozy Student Lounge for any available seat and spotted one in the far corner. She squeezed by some students she recognized from another a cappella group, saying hello as she passed, and settled in for the performance. It had been a full week since Jolene had spoken to Ellie in person. They had seen each other in class, but Jolene had been too late to get a seat next to Ellie. It might have been for the best, actually. She already had a hard enough time focusing in class, and the kiss in the Quad had only made things harder. Her ambivalence toward homework and class participation seemed to get worse each day, and recollections of Ellie constantly preoccupied her thoughts.

She glimpsed an unfamiliar member of the Jones Tones clothed in a black tunic dress and a bright turquoise hijab peeking out from behind the worn curtain to wave hello to a friend. The group members always wore black with a blue accessory. Most of the groups on campus had their own uniform for big events like this. Acapellago was very strict in their style, something that had always bothered Jolene. She didn't appreciate being forced to wear a matching cummerbund and bow tie to every event. Unfortunately, her fellow Acapellagoes were sticklers for tradition and their group had been dressing in the same style for over sixty years. It suddenly dawned on her that she would only have to wear the uniform twice more before her graduation. Maybe it wasn't so bad after all. She'd probably miss it the moment she put it back in the community box for the next new group member to use in the spring. The realization of how few performances she had left reminded her of how little time she had with Ellie. She had to make it count.

She glanced up at the clock, realizing the show was about to start. She switched her cell phone to vibrate and waited in anticipation for the lights to dim.

The Jones Tones came out of the side room to wild roars and bawdy cheers from the audience. Ellie filed in with the others, in a simple black dress that flared out from her waist with a blue neckerchief tied off to the side. She looked absolutely gorgeous. If Jolene had been unsure about her attraction before, it was clear as day now.

When the group began to sing, Jolene was instantly lost in the music. While she was happy to see some new faces among the Jones Tones, she had a hard time seeing anyone except Ellie. Her thoughts wandered back to her shy looks as they hunched over their project in the café. She remembered the night of their beatboxing lesson, when she had first realized the extent of Ellie's singing talent. She remembered the taste of Ellie's tongue in her mouth. There was so much that Jolene loved about her time with Ellie: her kind eyes and quiet encouragement, the friendly sparring and successful partnership, her beauty, and her determination. She thought of the few times she had caught Ellie blushing after she had muttered a witty comment with not-so-subtle sexual innuendo—comments that inclined her to pull the ever-present barrette out of Ellie's short hair and run her fingers through it, just to see if Ellie's eyes would slip closed at the feeling. She longed to kiss Ellie again, in absolute privacy, and to still her soft lips. She wanted to hear Ellie beatbox and sing just for her. She wanted all that, and more.

Jolene waited impatiently for the solo. Finally, the opening notes of *Can't Take My Eyes Off You* rang out over the crowd. With a steady beat, Ellie entered after the first few notes, clearly improved since her lesson. In fact, Jolene was mesmerized by Ellie's effort. From the movement of her lips to her left heel tapping out the downbeat, Ellie was captivating. When it was over, Jolene joined the rest of the audience in thunderous applause. She could hardly wait for the program to be over so she could congratulate Ellie on a job well done.

After the audience filed out, Jolene waited in front of the lounge. She caught sight of Ellie, hugging the soloist for Beyoncé's *Drunk in Love*. When she noticed Jolene, she quickly disentangled herself and walked over. She radiated pure joy.

"You came!" she exclaimed.

"Yes, of course. You were fantastic, Ellie!" It was the truth, after all.

"Thanks. I hardly remember it. It's all a blur," she admitted.

"Well, I'll never forget it," Jolene said.

"Really?"

Jolene readied herself, as she put on a brave face, complete with a small grin. *Here goes nothing*, she decided. "Yeah, I couldn't take my eyes off you. You're just too good to be true."

When Ellie didn't respond immediately, Jolene regretted her sad attempt at flirting. But, before she could imagine how to backpedal, Ellie laughed.

"Oh, wow, what a cheesy thing to say!" she said between breathless chuckles.

Jolene shrugged before answering. "I will admit that's pretty cheesy, but it *did* make you smile."

Ellie's laughter subsided, but her delighted expression stayed put.

"So," she began.

"So?" Jolene responded

"What are you doing now that you've been serenaded by the best a cappella group on campus?" Ellie asked slyly.

"Oh, that's rich! How can you say that to the person that taught you everything you know?" Jolene replied with amusement.

"I don't know if you taught me everything," she said.

Jolene wanted to jump at that remark with something devilish.

"Maybe not, but there's always more to learn," she replied instead.

"Is there? What are you going to teach me next?"

Jolene was surprised to see Ellie like this. Singing in front of a crowd obviously boosted her confidence, so she decided to press her luck. "I don't know, but we could discuss it while I walk you home. I mean, if you don't have anything else planned," Jolene offered.

"I'm all yours." She beamed. "Let me just grab my coat."

They meandered slowly toward Ellie's dorm, their hands occasionally bumping while they walked. They walked in step together across campus and talked about the performance. Ellie asked for Jolene's opinions on each song in order, a quirk that made Jolene's heart leap because, of course, Ellie would want to deconstruct everything in order. As they passed by the Campus Center, their hands gently brushed again. Jolene held onto Ellie's pinkie finger this time, determined to get another chance to hold Ellie's warm hand. A moment passed before their fingers intertwined, a motion that now felt second nature. She answered Ellie's questions about the performance truthfully, letting her know that the Jones Tones newest protégé wasn't really as good as everyone believed. She had been flat for half a verse in her solo and had completely bombed her audition with Acapellago at the beginning of the year. But, she had to admit that the audience seemed to enjoy it, and most people didn't care about pitch as much as Jolene. Ellie joked easily about the comments, taking them in stride. She shared the newest backstage gossip about Sylvia and Alyssa that seemed to explode just in time for their biggest performance of the semester. Jolene loved hearing that other groups struggled to keep everyone in line.

A silence settled between them as they reached the crosswalk. "Thank you for inviting me. I'm really glad you gave me a chance to help you," Jolene said.

"I'm glad I did too," Ellie replied.

The autumn chill made their breath cloud and produced a ruddiness on Ellie's cheeks. When the dorm came into view, Ellie let go of Jolene's hand and searched her coat pocket for her keycard. Jolene instantly felt a small emptiness at the loss of touch, remembering the last time Ellie had shut the door on her. Before she could say anything, Ellie unlocked the door and motioned for Jolene to enter.

"After you, coach," she joked.

They walked up the two flights to Ellie's room. Jolene examined a collage of images taped to the door as Ellie rifled through her key ring. There were two photos of Ellie with the Jones Tones, one with them all dressed as animals. But the door was mostly covered with magazine clippings, many of them movie stars, including a lot of the female cast members from *Buffy the Vampire Slayer*. Jolene chuckled at that, but had to admit that she also harbored a crush for many of them. There was only one person she didn't recognize.

"Who's that?" Jolene asked as Ellie unlocked the door.

Ellie glanced at the door. "Oh, that's Thelma Golden," she offered. The name meant nothing to Jolene. Ellie took off her coat. "Yeah, she's not really famous outside her field, unfortunately. She's the Director and Chief Curator at The Studio Museum in Harlem. I keep her there to motivate me when I'm on my way to class in the morning. Her career path has been such an inspiration to me. She went to a women's college too."

Ellie kicked off her heels and motioned for Jolene to come in. Jolene closed the door and took in the small room around her. It was cozy, with twinkling Christmas lights draped over the window and bed. The picture motif on the door continued throughout the room, with a few movie posters—*West Side Story* and *Love, Actually*—and lots of pictures of Ellie and her friends at Jones. Jolene inspected the corkboard, pinned with ticket stubs and greeting cards. When she turned around, Ellie was sitting on the edge of her bed.

"Like what you see?"

Jolene's thoughts stuttered for a moment at the question.

"Yes. I do," she said, her mouth dry.

Ellie's lips quirked up. "Come here."

She sat next to Ellie. Their hands found each other, as if by habit, and Jolene started brushing her thumb across one of Ellie's knuckles.

"You were great tonight," Jolene whispered.

"Thanks. I couldn't have done it without you."

"That was all you, Ellie."

Jolene reached up to touch Ellie's chin with her free hand and let the pad of her thumb press into the tiny dimple there, only visible at close range. Ellie was nervously licking her lips; Jolene took the opportunity and leaned in.

As their lips met, Jolene's heart pounded. Ellie's fingers brushed across her collarbone and the memory of their last kiss flooded her. She wrapped her arms around Ellie's back and pressed their bodies tight. She felt Ellie breathe in sharply between kisses and realized it was laughter.

"What are you giggling about?" Jolene whispered against Ellie's cheek.

"Nothing. I'm just so happy you helped me with my beatboxing," she answered breathlessly as Jolene kissed her throat, nosing at the neckerchief still in place from the performance.

"I thought you might be giggling at my smooth moves," she murmured between kisses.

"I'd never joke about them!"

"Good. Then let me try a few more," she said, pulling the barrette out of Ellie's hair, just as she had envisioned while Ellie was on stage. Her hair was as soft as she had imagined. Jolene's hands wandered, at first through the short hair at the nape of Ellie's neck and then coming to the silk neckerchief. Jolene untied the scarf and let it drop onto the bed beside them. She pressed her lips against the newly revealed skin, and felt her pulse quicken. Ellie's soft gasp reassured Jolene that she was in just the right spot.

"God, Jolene, that feels amazing."

Jolene hummed against Ellie's warm skin, and felt the other girl's hands move through her long hair as she continued kissing and licking the steadily throbbing pulse point. Ellie squirmed against her mouth and hands before pressing Jolene back onto the bed.

Jolene broke the kiss. "Hold on," she said.

Ellie pulled back. "Are you okay? Am I rushing you?" she asked.

"No! No, it's great. It's just my shoes. I don't want to get your bed dirty."

When Ellie looked at her with utter exasperation, Jolene shrugged helplessly. Ellie quickly unzipped the heavy boots and dropped them onto the floor.

"Better?" Ellie asked, one eyebrow raised.

"Much better," Jolene answered.

She pulled Ellie close again and let a hand wander to Ellie's thigh where she felt the smooth skin that continued up underneath that beautiful black dress. Her fingers longed to explore.

"Ellie?" she managed to ask between breathless kisses.

"Yeah?"

"Can I unzip you?"

Jolene watched Ellie's chest rise and fall. Her breasts were straining against the fabric with each quick breath. She looked deeply into Ellie's eyes, waiting for her response.

"Yes, please," she said.

Ellie turned around and situated herself between Jolene's legs. Slowly, Jolene unzipped the dress, relishing every inch it revealed and saw a delicate lace bra crossing the V-shaped sliver of skin. She leaned in to trail kisses along Ellie's spine, paying careful attention to the sharp shoulder blades on either side.

"Once you take this dress off me, it's going to be very one-sided nudity," Ellie remarked.

"Well, you can return the favor in a second."

As Jolene slowly lifted the dress over Ellie's head, the scratch of the underskirt crinkled against her skin. She dropped it to the floor, leaving Ellie between her legs, her back exposed.

"I love this," Jolene said, her fingers tracing along the black lace. She saw Ellie shiver at the touch.

"I'd love it even more if you took it off me," Ellie said coyly.

Jolene unfastened the bra and watched with hungry eyes as Ellie maneuvered out of it and threw it across the room. Jolene found the tiny freckles that spread out across the pale skin under her fingers sexy and beautiful, just like Ellie. She inhaled deeply and wrapped her arms around Ellie's middle, embracing her in a hug as she leaned her forehead against Ellie's neck. Jolene matched her breathing to the woman pressed against her, soaking in the feel of being so close.

"I think it's my turn now," Ellie said, her voice a little rough from the singing. Jolene released Ellie and leaned back, unsure of how Ellie wanted to undress her. When Ellie turned, the shadows from the twinkle lights illuminated her curves. Jolene let herself look. The waistband of her matching lace panties met the small swell of her stomach, and a belly button that Jolene wanted to kiss immediately. Ellie's breasts were just as smooth and beautiful as the rest of her, but Jolene's eyes ended up fixed on her collarbone, mesmerized by the sharp edges beneath the thin skin there and the dusting of freckles that looked so inviting. Ellie reached out, her fingers dancing along the hemline of Jolene's long-sleeved sweater, before slowly pulling it up to reveal the thin tank top underneath. Jolene let her arms rise above her head, smiling as the shirt caught on her hair. Ellie tugged, laughing in frustration, before throwing it onto the floor beside her dress.

"Too many layers," she whispered.

"Baby, it's cold outside," Jolene offered with a smirk.

"It's too early for Christmas music references! I want fall to last forever." Ellie swatted playfully at Jolene's now bare arm.

"Hm. Big fan of the pumpkin spice latte?" Jolene asked.

"No. I make far too many of them at the café. But I am a big fan of you," Ellie answered.

"Hey. That's my line! You were the one with the big solo tonight," Jolene responded with a snort. Ellie moved in, kissing Jolene deeply, her fingers still tracing along the edges of the tank top.

Jolene pulled back for some air.

"Trying to quiet me with a kiss?"

"Yes. Arms up!" Ellie ordered.

Jolene did as she was asked. Ellie stripped off the shirt, leaving her simple black sports bra behind. Jolene noticed her nipples poking up against the elastic material. Ellie's eyes lingered there, and then brushed them both with a light touch.

Her eyelids dropped.

"Is this okay?" she asked.

"Yeah. Don't stop, please," Jolene begged. Her stomach tightened as Ellie cupped her breasts through the material, still rubbing at the hardened flesh. Jolene craved the touch, but she wanted more of it and she wanted it everywhere.

"Oh, forget this," Jolene said in frustration as she lifted the bra over her head.

"Better?" Ellie asked, amused.

"Oh, yeah," she said as she let her own hands begin to wander along Ellie's body. They both explored with fleeting touches, never stopping at one place for too long between the occasional kiss. The heat between them intensified. When Ellie pushed her back against the pillows, Jolene laughed.

"What?" Ellie asked.

"I think you like being in charge."

"Didn't you figure that out from our project?" Ellie asked innocently.

"Yes. But it's nice to see you commit to it in other aspects of your life too."

Ellie kissed her again, slipping her tongue between Jolene's parted lips. She didn't mind when Ellie paused the conversation this way.

After a few minutes, Ellie's caresses ebbed. Jolene followed suit, realizing that sex was probably not in the cards at the moment. She still had so much to learn about Ellie. The last thing she wanted was for this to be a one-time only thing. She exhaled deeply as Ellie slipped off of her. She immediately missed the weight of Ellie pressing into her, so she curled onto her side, looking into her bright blue eyes and stroking her hair.

"You're beautiful, Ellie."

"Thanks, but now how am I supposed to compliment your amazing looks without it feeling redundant?" she asked softly as she pressed a kiss to Jolene's wrist.

"You could always sing *Can't Take My Eyes Off You*," Jolene giggled.

Ellie joined in, her eyes crinkling in delight.

Jolene could talk to Ellie all night but had to ask the question. "Are you tired?"

Ellie paused, clearly torn. "No."

"Are you fibbing?"

"Yes," she admitted after a second.

"Thought so," Jolene said as she pressed a quick kiss to Ellie's nose. "A cappella can do that to the best of us."

They held each other close for a few long minutes.

"Will you stay?" Ellie asked quietly.

"If you want me to."

"I want you to. Very, very much."

Ellie sat up quickly and hopped off the bed. She picked up her crumpled dress, plugged in her phone, and grabbed another blanket from the armchair in the corner. Jolene let her eyes glide over Ellie again, determined to memorize it all—the toes with sparkling nail polish, the tiny blackish bruise on her knee, the softly padded stomach, the oddly shaped scar on her triceps, the perfectly pink nipples—the list was long. Ellie turned out the lights and slipped into bed.

"You can take off your jeans if you'd be more comfy that way." Jolene, who had almost forgotten they were still on, wiggled out of them and tossed them beside the bed.

Ellie pulled up an extra blanket and turned to face Jolene.

"Are you a big spoon or a little spoon?" Jolene asked.

Ellie shrugged. "I don't think I've ever been a spoon before."

"Well, you're a little pushy, so you might be the big spoon, but you're also shorter than me, so you might be the little spoon."

"Pushy!" Ellie protested at the mock indignation.

"Yes. But I like that about you," she said, pressing a quick kiss to Ellie's cheek.

"Hmm, well just for that you have to be the big spoon tonight," Ellie announced as she turned away and scooted her ass into Jolene's belly.

Jolene draped an arm over Ellie's waist and soaked in the feeling of someone in her arms. Jessica had never let her stay the night; they hadn't really been the cuddly types. She and Ellie hadn't even had sex yet but she already felt more of a connection than she ever had with Jessica. They felt right together, even from that first class discussion on the political history of Hawaii. Ellie sighed, apparently content to be the "little spoon."

"I'm so glad you came to my concert tonight."

"Me too."

CHAPTER FIFTEEN

Something's different.

Ellie's eyes blinked open toward the ceiling, covered with tiny star stickers left behind by someone who occupied the room before her. Ellie intended to do the same when she graduated. She hoped a future student might remember to reach for the stars—or something equally motivational—even if the idea sounded cheesy beyond belief. They had certainly helped her once or twice over the years and she wasn't embarrassed to admit it. But this morning she could only look at the messy rainbow-colored constellations with wonder. She felt a warm breath ghost across her shoulder. Jolene had really spent the night.

Jolene was still asleep. Ellie marveled that, thanks to the beautiful, inquisitive woman beside her, she had delivered her best performance to date. And, more than that, something about her beatboxing performance at the concert the previous evening had freed her and given her confidence a much-needed boost. Ellie felt her own breaths get shallow when she pictured what had happened after that. The soft touches, warm words, and gentle kisses were fantastic memories that Ellie hoped she would remember forever. It had been bliss, but too brief; Ellie wanted it to go on forever.

Jolene's arm rested across her bare torso. Ellie sensed heat pool in her body, aching for the fingers to move up the few inches to cup her breast. Unfortunately, despite her wishes, Jolene still slumbered peacefully.

Ellie glanced at the clock. Her body was so used to waking up at seven thirty that even a woman draped across her couldn't change that. She let herself fall back into the warmth that surrounded her. Her eyes wandered across black hair and sharp cheekbones for a few pleasurable minutes before they slipped closed.

Ellie awoke again when Jolene began to shift into consciousness. Another glance at the clock proved to Ellie that she could, in fact, fall back to sleep under certain circumstances. She let her eyes trace over Jolene's sleepy gaze and mussed hair.

"Good morning."

Jolene yawned and rolled her shoulders. "What time is it?" she asked.

"Still early," Ellie answered quietly. "Got any plans for the day?"

She hoped that Jolene would be free to stay in her arms all day. Her desire for Jolene was deepening acutely. She wanted more contact, more kissing, more talking—more Jolene.

"Not really," Jolene replied gently. "And even if I did, I'm too warm right now."

"Same here."

Ellie kissed lightly at Jolene's pliable lips. In a few heartbeats the kiss grew more passionate, proving that neither of them would fall back to sleep anytime soon. Their tongues twisted together until Jolene finally moved her fingers up and over the swell of Ellie's aching breast. Filled with desire, Ellie breathed hard into the touch and heard herself moan into their kiss.

"Please, don't stop," she murmured as Jolene moved her thumb across the erect nipple. She squirmed at the new sensation before Jolene pushed back the covers and exposed both of their bodies to the cool morning air. Ellie felt a shiver run along her skin, but wasn't sure if it was the air or Jolene's firm hands on her breasts. She reached up and pulled on a loose strand of Jolene's long black hair.

"You're so gorgeous," Jolene whispered as she quickly straddled Ellie.

Ellie leaned up to capture that beautiful mouth. She ran her fingers along Jolene's hairline, guiding her lips downward to her own sensitive neck. Each kiss, wetter than the last, heightened waves of anticipation and desire that made Ellie tremble. Jolene traced her lips from Ellie's neck down to the center of her chest and, teasingly, lingered there. Ellie was desperate for Jolene's mouth on her full, heaving breasts. Ellie muffled a curse when Jolene finally took a nipple into her warm mouth and suckled it softly.

"Feel good?" Jolene asked, breath hot against the hardened nipple.

When Ellie moved her hips up to brush against Jolene, she let out a gasp that promised pleasure. Ellie tangled her fingers in Jolene's long hair, who sucked harder, first one nipple, and then the other. She shuddered at the small flicks of Jolene's tongue across her skin, but she felt like a pillow queen from all the attention.

"My turn," she said with a grin, before rolling them both over. Jolene flopped her head back onto the pillow. Ellie paused a moment to take in the sight before her. Jolene's hair was fanned out, creating a beautiful pitch-colored backdrop for her tanned skin. Her smile was stuck in place and her bare body looked absolutely magnificent. She couldn't wait another second to taste Jolene's skin and mouth at all the tiny beauty marks that dotted her skin. She wanted to create new constellations with them.

Ellie grazed along Jolene's ear. "You are the most beautiful woman," she whispered.

She brushed her fingers along the swell of Jolene's side, captivated by the feeling of such an athletic body beneath her. She licked along the collarbone jutting from beneath the almond skin and heard Jolene's noises of pleasure in response. Her next fascination was with Jolene's delicate breasts. She let her nose rub over one hardened nub and then sucked it into her mouth. Jolene encouraged the attention with a guiding hand in her hair. Ellie swirled her tongue in small motions while mimicking the motion with her hand on Jolene's other breast, nipping lightly. She felt Jolene's hips start to roll lightly against her body. Ellie wanted to whimper at the feel, her own body telling her to move to relieve the building tension.

Her affection for Jolene was no match for the intense arousal that consumed her every thought as she moved further down the lithe body lying beneath her. She licked along the center of Jolene's belly, dipping her tongue into the cute belly button blocking her intended path to what waited beyond. She heard Jolene suck in sharply. She lingered there and then continued down to a hip. She grabbed firmly, and started licking at the spot where flesh met bone. Jolene's hips bucked up against Ellie's chest in response and a hiss sounded out across the silent room.

Happy to see that Jolene was sensitive in other places, she moved to the other hip, brushing one hand across the panties still in place from the night before.

"Can I take these off?" she asked, looking up to meet Jolene's half-closed eyes.

"Yes," came the quick reply.

She kissed at the cotton fabric before hooking her thumbs over the top and pulling them down and off Jolene's long legs. Ellie swung her leg back over Jolene's thighs.

She felt one of Jolene's strong legs shift from under her body and hummed when their hips slotted together. Even through her own panties, she could feel the heat radiating from Jolene's pelvis. She bucked hard into Jolene and was glad to hear her moan into their kiss. She continued moving her tongue against Jolene's as she let one hand slip down, pinching a nipple between her fingers. Her other hand brushed lightly over the hair at Jolene's groin. It was long enough to run her fingers through, a realization that thrilled Ellie. She definitely liked the idea of something to hold onto down there.

Jolene's bucking quickly became more insistent.

"More, please," Jolene begged in between deep gulps of air.

Ellie answered the plea by licking two fingers before moving them down to rub soft circles against Jolene's wetness, moving her fingers faster as she circled her other hand around to grab Jolene's perfect ass. Ellie shivered with pleasure as Jolene clutched desperately at both of her breasts, but Ellie refused to be distracted. She ran her teeth along Jolene's collarbone; two last strokes against the wet heat between her thighs drove Jolene to the lovely, fiery rhythm of orgasm.

Ellie pressed an ear to the top of Jolene's breast to hear the loud thumping of her heartbeat slowly returning to something resembling normal as she wrapped her arms around the gorgeous woman that had captured her heart. It was minutes later before Jolene managed to blink back to awareness.

"Oh, man," Jolene offered shakily, "how am I going to compete with that?"

"Don't worry, I'm easy," Ellie answered.

Jolene quirked an eyebrow at the challenge.

"Wait, no, I mean…"

Before Ellie could backpedal, Jolene was laughing. Ellie shook her head in delight as Jolene pushed her onto her back and climbed on top. It was amazing they hadn't rolled out of the small twin bed yet.

Jolene separated Ellie's thighs and nosed at the center of the lacy panties.

"You're so wet," Jolene murmured.

Ellie could only nod. She had never been this aroused in her life. Jolene's pleasure had driven her crazy, and now the feel of the expert tongue that had explored her mouth all morning against the wet fabric was almost too much. Jolene took a detour to kiss both of Ellie's heavy thighs, spending careful seconds to trace along the stretch marks all pointing back toward the heat pooling in Ellie's groin.

She moved a hand down to cover them, but Jolene just kissed her fingertips instead.

"They're beautiful, just like the rest of you."

Their eyes met and Ellie knew it wasn't some line. Jolene was being honest and that was more pleasing than anything she had done with her mouth or fingers. She moved her hand away and grabbed the back of Jolene's neck instead. Jolene returned to lick at the fine stripes along her skin, making her whole body ache with desire and her thighs quiver erratically. One hand brushed at the wet spot again while the other glided back up to one of her nipples. Her hips began bucking, her body eager for more contact. Jolene breathed something that sounded like *impatient* under her breath before stripping off the underwear. Without the fabric, the sensation was intensified. Ellie surrendered to Jolene's insistence. Her eyes fluttered closed and sounds came from her lips that no one else had ever pulled from her before. Soon, she was grinding against Jolene's tongue with three fingers pressed inside her. The white heat of her orgasm rushed across her body as everything came together perfectly—fingers brushing inside her, a talented tongue rubbing circles over her sensitive clit and another hand pinching at a tender nipple. She heard herself moan Jolene's name as she grabbed at the sheets. It was blinding and beautiful and she never wanted to come down.

CHAPTER SIXTEEN

Get out of bed!

Jolene awoke and pushed back the covers. For the first time in weeks—and not because of class—she felt motivated. She padded over to her closet, certain of what to wear. Her favorite button-down shirt and worn-in jeans had gotten many compliments in the past and, hopefully, today would only add to that list.

Jolene still felt like she was walking on clouds. For the last three days, her encounter with Ellie had replayed over and over. Every waking moment was consumed with the memory of Ellie's freckles on creamy skin, or her short hair catching on the edge of her eyebrow. She had found herself zoning out again and again, thinking of the sounds Ellie made when she kissed her in the exact right spot or Ellie's fingers grasping at the sheets.

She shook herself from the memories, knowing that today was not the day for lollygagging. Jolene slipped on her clothes and stepped in front of the mirror. She rubbed at her face, and breathed out slowly. It had been a long time since she had been so carefree and excited. Even Mo and Natalie had noticed the change. She, of course, had told them the whole story the moment she got home from her day with Ellie. Mo begged for more details, while Natalie nodded perceptively. She could tell that they were both happy for her. When she had asked them for advice about her plan they had jumped at the chance to help. They had crowded together in Natalie's room until the early hours of the morning making sure that Jolene's plan was perfect. Jolene turned from the mirror and grabbed her bag. She couldn't be late. On her way out the door, she grabbed a granola bar and high-fived the picture of Elizabeth Warren taped by her light switch. *Give me strength*, she thought.

In a matter of minutes, Jolene was seated in Ellie's usual seat for Mehra's SWaG class. Her knee jumped while she watched students filter into the classroom, looking for Ellie. When Ellie finally did arrive, she stopped just inside the doorway when she saw Jolene in the second row, something that obviously surprised her.

"Excuse me, miss. I think you're in my seat," Ellie chided.

Jolene glanced up at the woman that had cracked her heart wide open, before answering. "I know. I have a theory that people who sit in this seat always get amazing grades. I wanted to test it out."

"I think it's the student that gets the grades!" Ellie replied grumpily.

"I can make it up to you, though."

"Oh yeah?" Ellie asked as she slid into the open seat next to Jolene. "And how are you going to do that?"

Jolene reached into the bag by her feet to pull out a CD, and handed it over to Ellie who was watching suspiciously.

"What's this?" Ellie asked. "More beatboxing tutorials? I thought we were past that. I'm a master at it now," she joked.

"No, not that. As a child of the nineties, I felt it was only right to give you a mixtape as my way of asking you to be my girlfriend," she explained.

She watched Ellie try to bite down on her smile.

"I don't know why I ever thought you were a cool girl. You are clearly the biggest goofball at this college," Ellie said.

"You thought I was a cool?"

"Yeah, past tense. I know better now," Ellie quipped.

Jolene clutched at her heart and feigned pain.

"Ouch El!"

"Well, I'm seriously considering saying yes, but I need to know what songs are on here first. Your music taste is definitely a determining factor here," Ellie replied.

"Obviously," Jolene agreed, taking the track list out of her notebook.

She watched Ellie scan the titles and knew she, despite the "help" of Natalie and Mo, had chosen correctly. Ellie was grinning ear to ear.

"Well?" she asked hopefully.

At that moment, Professor Mehra glided into the classroom, exactly on time as usual, wearing a patterned pantsuit that would make Hillary Clinton weep for joy. Jolene silently cursed her, for not giving them one extra minute this morning.

"Good morning everyone," she greeted.

Jolene waited impatiently until Mehra opened a PowerPoint halfway through the class period. While she fussed with the projector, Ellie leaned over, her lips brushing Jolene's ear.

"My answer is yes."

Ellie's joyous expression was the only thing she could focus on. The warmth blooming beneath her chest felt like fire. She reached out and squeezed Ellie's fingers once before drawing her hand back. They couldn't both be distracted for the rest of the class period. Jolene let her thoughts drift away while she imagined her new life as a girlfriend. And her new life with a girlfriend! Excitement caused her knee to bounce and her fingers to grow restless. Her nonchalant demeanor slipped away as she allowed the endless possibilities to spring to mind. She could feel the goofy look etched on her face, but she didn't even try to quash it. She had a girlfriend!

CHAPTER SEVENTEEN

This must be a new record.

Ellie leaned back, happy that the rehearsal had ended without any drama. The Jones Tones had gone a whole week without a giant meltdown. It proved they were still professional when everyone worked together. Ellie was happy to see the newer members still excited about their performances at the jam. They had a newfound confidence that would only make them stronger group members as time went by.

"You look happy." Gabrielle was perched on the arm of the chair beside her. The junior had rocked her solo at the jam, which proved yet again that she was future president material, despite only being in the group for a little over a year. Sometimes the late bloomers turned out to be the best group members.

"I *am* happy," Ellie answered easily as she let her eyes slip closed again.

"About Sylvia and Alyssa holding it together?" Gabrielle asked.

"Yeah. That's one reason."

"What's the other?" she prodded.

"I have a new girlfriend."

"Ooo! Tell me all about her!"

"She's in another a cappella group," Ellie said, cracking an eye open to see the response.

"No! How *dare* you!" Gabrielle clasped a hand to her chest. "Is she any good?" she whispered behind her hand.

"She's amazing. And not just when she's singing!"

"Boom. There it is!" Gabrielle laughed. "Seriously though, tell me more."

Ellie launched into the story of how she and Jolene had slowly worked their way up from group project partners to girlfriends. She told Gabrielle about their first date and the last-minute kiss, pleased at her friend's enthusiasm. They had only been an official couple for a week, but everything felt so perfect. Ellie hoped the honeymoon phase would never end.

"So, what group is she in?"

"Acapellago," Ellie answered.

"Is she the one that helped you with your beatboxing for the jam?"

"Yeah, that's sort of how it all got started."

"I've always said that a cappella changes lives!" Gabrielle joked. "But, really, I'm so happy for you. God knows we need someone in a stable relationship in this group—even if it is with the enemy. I've had enough of Sylvia and Alyssa. Were they always like this?"

Ellie thought back to their first year in the Jones Tones. "No, I don't think it got bad until after Alyssa went abroad last year. They've always been a bit rocky, but I think Sylvia feels like she got left behind. If the rumor mill is right, then Alyssa hooked up with some people while she was abroad."

"That's probably the root of all these fights they have now," Gabrielle added. "I don't think they're both going to last the year at this rate."

"Hopefully, there are more rehearsals like this. They both clearly love performances. I guess time will tell," Ellie murmured.

Gabrielle got up from her perch. "It sure will! I'm going to head home. I'll see you after Thanksgiving."

Ellie dug her phone out of her bag. She started to type out a message for Jolene, but wondered if it would disturb her while she tried to wrestle with the pile of homework they all seemed to get just before a holiday.

No fight at rehearsal tonight! :)

A few seconds later, the phone buzzed a response from her girlfriend. Jolene's name on the screen was enough to make her light up. She never pictured herself as a hopeless romantic, but each day proved that she had the potential to turn into that person.

That's a first! Glad it went well. Will you come over and finish this paper for me?

Ellie knew how frustrated Jolene must be if her first thought was to complain about homework. Usually, she would make some witty comments about the superiority of Acapellago or reference some other musical group that had difficult members. Fleetwood Mac seemed to be a favorite. She sent her reply.

That's against the Honor Code.

Her phone buzzed again.

I know. Mo loves to lecture me about it all the time. Downside of having a friend on Honor Board. She'd snitch on me.

Ellie felt buoyant as she got up from her chair. But it was time she got started on her own work. There was only one day left before fall break and she had plenty to finish before then. A pang of sadness settled over her about the upcoming holiday. For the third year in a row, she wouldn't see her family over the long weekend. She had tried to go home for Thanksgiving in her first year, but it had been a disaster. The memory of disappointment written clearly on her father's face during that week brought tears to her eyes. Her high school experience had been rough, from start to finish. Ellie still wished that she could forget it all. Between the bullies that had honed in on her weight fluctuations to the boyfriends that had been a little too aggressive, her memories felt like a solid weight that tried to keep her down. She had channeled all the hurt from that time of her life into her schoolwork, which was part of the reason she had been accepted to Jones University. Her grades were nearly perfect by her senior year in high school, but it still wasn't enough to win her parents' approval. They envisioned a future so different from the one she wanted—one mostly comprised of a job in finance or something equally "stable" and a wealthy man that would be good husband material. The breaking point had been during that first fall break after weeks of building up the courage to come out as bisexual to her family. She had known her true feelings from the start of high school, but had been too scared to talk about them with anyone until after she started to see the clear acceptance everywhere at Jones. So, with her friends' kind words and support ringing in her ears, she had traveled home for that first Thanksgiving. But her mother's tears and father's insistence that it was just a phase had felt like a knife through her chest. They still talked on the phone monthly, although it could be stilted and uncomfortable. The rift had left her reeling and alone. She still went home for the summer between her internships, but it had been years since she had felt a deep connection to her family. They were only a few hours away in the suburbs of Boston, but she had never felt more distant.

The phone buzzed in her hand again, and Ellie pushed aside the painful memories.

See you at lunch tomorrow? I wanna give you a really sloppy kiss before I leave.

She smiled, thoughts consumed with how lucky she was in this moment. She didn't need approval from her family because she knew that the affection she had for Jolene was beautiful and real. That was all that mattered, in the end. She didn't need anyone else to tell her it was a good thing. She knew it.

Yes! I'll take a sloppy kiss any day! :)

She put her phone away and resigned herself to a long night of homework and two more classes before she could get that promised kiss, even though it was the last one she'd get for almost a week. She had contemplated Jolene's offer to go with her to New Hampshire for Thanksgiving, but decided it was definitely too soon to meet Jolene's family. They were still new as a couple and it seemed risky. Plus, she realized, Rose would kill her if she skipped out on Thanksgiving. It was now practically a tradition that they celebrated together. This would probably be her last opportunity to experience the hilarity of getting to witness Rose struggle to cook a turkey big enough to feed all of the café workers that she seemed to adopt over the holidays. The thought of the previous year's debacle left her excited to see what would transpire this time around. It would be for the best if she were there with the fire extinguisher again, just in case.

CHAPTER EIGHTEEN

Just a few more steps and then you're home free.

Jolene took a deep breath as she walked up the staircase. She sidestepped the dog curled on the top step before turning down the hallway toward her bedroom and heaved a deep sigh. This wasn't her bedroom. Not really. Jolene had grown up in New Mexico, but as soon as she left for college on the East Coast, her family decided to pack up everything and leave her childhood home behind. Her self-proclaimed hippie parents had donated most of her things to charity during her second semester at Jones University. She looked in the room that was "hers." There were two pieces of art on the beige wall, neither of which she had ever seen before. Only one stuffed animal had made it to New Hampshire with the move. Her raggedy cat, Smiley, had been her closest companion growing up. There was still so much she missed about her home in New Mexico.

More than the comforts of home, she missed her grandparents. They had debated about moving east as well, but decided, at the last moment, to stay behind with the bookstore they had owned for over forty years. In times like these, she felt the distance between them the most. Her extended family wasn't complete without them at the dinner table.

Jolene threw another sweatshirt on before jumping under the covers and moving her feet around to warm the bed. She opened her laptop and connected to the extremely slow Internet. She was supposed to Skype with Ellie in five minutes.

Jolene closed her eyes. Thanksgiving vacation was difficult. Her parents were great and loving, and always had been. They had supported her through everything, even her experimental year in high school when she had tried out blue hair for a summer. Their support when she came out as a lesbian still ranked as one of her fondest memories of them as a family. It was at that moment that she understood the meaning of unconditional love. Unfortunately, her relatives were a different story. Her handful of aunts and uncles rotated hosting Thanksgiving and this just happened to be her parents' year, only making it more stressful to be home. Jolene felt like it was impossible to escape their scrutiny. The constant barrage of questions about her career path and schoolwork was too much. She had long since memorized the conversation that each family member over the age of forty relied on when they saw her during the holiday season. She could answer the questions in her sleep at this point.

Senior year. American Studies with a concentration in politics. No, I'm actually graduating early. Still applying at this point. No, I don't have a boyfriend.

She rubbed at her eyes, and chose to focus on the bright point of her day—Ellie. Her conversations with Ellie each night had been wonderful. Even though they were a few hours apart, Jolene's desire for her hadn't wavered in the slightest. If anything, her devotion to Ellie was deepening. The invitation popped up on her screen before she had more time to consider that fact.

"Hi!" came Ellie's bright voice. Jolene could see Ellie's colorful dorm room, but her girlfriend was nowhere to be seen.

"Hello, phantom voice," she quipped.

"Sorry! I'm just putting on my PJs!"

"You're supposed to be taking clothes off when you Skype your girlfriend," Jolene replied casually, trying not to give away that she was a little horny. Being unable to touch Ellie was only getting harder as each day passed.

"I never got that memo," Ellie responded as she sank down into her desk chair. Her short hair was piled into a cute little knot at the top of her head. Jolene could only stare in wonder at her girlfriend. She felt her chest tighten at the thought of being in that room next to Ellie.

"How was your day? Get any homework done?" she asked.

Ellie rested her chin on her hand. "Absolutely not. That's what this weekend is for," she answered.

"Well, if you don't do a little homework how are you going to squeeze me into your busy schedule this weekend when I get back?" Jolene teased. She had her own homework to do too. The senior slide was holding her back, yet again.

"Oh, I'll make time for you."

"That's so sweet," Jolene said.

"Anything for my favorite girl. You look chilly."

Jolene looked at herself in the corner of her own screen. The comforter covered most of her face, and the hood of her sweatshirt covered her hair. She was definitely bundled into a nest.

"It's cold here!" she grumbled.

"Missing New Mexico?"

"Tell me about it."

"At least the trip is shorter! No airport security and all that crap," Ellie offered.

"Yeah, it's still not the same," Jolene agreed through her pile of blankets.

Ellie frowned. "I know. What do you miss most about it?" she asked.

"It seems like everyone I remember from high school is home for Thanksgiving this year and I keep seeing all their photos online. I just wish I could be there instead of here," Jolene said.

"You don't see them very often now that you're on the East Coast, huh?"

"No. And I barely talk to them online anymore. I guess losing touch with people is normal, but I feel like a bad friend."

"You're not! It's totally normal. You shouldn't worry about it. I mean, I might be biased, but I think you are a great friend and an even better girlfriend. I think lots of people would agree."

"Thanks El. I've never had complaints in the girlfriend department before. It's nice to hear you think the same."

Jolene saw Ellie's eyes dart away from the computer screen. Maybe that wasn't the best thing to say. Ellie's limited dating experience, she realized, might make her own past seem intimidating. When they had discussed previous relationships while Jolene had packed her bags for fall break, she had noticed that Ellie's demeanor became increasingly subdued. Jolene had mentioned her three ex-girlfriends, including her high school sweetheart, and wondered whether Ellie's anxiety over the subject was jealousy or a feeling of inadequacy. Of course, Jolene was completely content, but she didn't know how to assure Ellie of this fact. Mentioning it only seemed to make Ellie pull back more quickly, protective of her emotions.

"Anyway!" Jolene started, steering the conversation away from the careless misstep she'd made. "What are your plans for Thanksgiving dinner tomorrow?"

"Ah. I haven't decided yet. Either delivery from Mr. Wok or delivery from Four Star Pizza," she joked, seemingly relieved at the change of subject.

Jolene shook her head. "That's not a real Thanksgiving!" she chided.

"I'm just kidding. That's what I'll be doing the day after Thanksgiving. I'm looking forward to going over to Rose's tomorrow. Her little Orphan Thanksgiving for the café workers is always fun and/or dangerous," Ellie explained.

"That'll be nice. Try not to get your eyebrows singed off."

"Yeah, I'll try to stay away from any fires that spring up. I think I'm going to bring Oreos as a gift," she mused, writing it down on a sticky note to remember in the morning. "Maybe that'll get me out of oven-tending duties."

Ellie had described Rose's love of the cookie during one of their date nights that ended with milkshakes at the café. They took turns sipping from the straw while they sat at the counter. Rose had puttered around and asked detailed questions about Jolene's life. Jolene repressed a laugh at the embarrassing stories Rose had shared about Ellie's nights in the café.

"Are you going to have time for a date tomorrow night?" Jolene asked.

She wrinkled her nose. "I don't think so. I have a feeling Rose is going to make me stay and do dishes because"—Ellie threw out some air quotes—"I'm so 'good' at it."

She was glad Ellie would be spending the night with friends. She knew a little about Ellie's home life, but only enough to recognize that she didn't have any mature, supportive women in her life, which was just one of the reasons she spent the holidays at Jones. She hoped that when they were back together they could have a long talk about it. Jolene made a mental note to swipe some of her mother's good Oolong tea. Everything was better with a warm cup in your hands.

"How was your family tonight?" Ellie asked before moving off screen again.

"Better. My cousin from Minnesota showed up today, so we spent most of the day chatting together. He's a really cool kid. Sophomore in college and completely different than his parents. I told him about you."

Ellie popped her head back in front of the camera. "Really? I thought you weren't out to anyone in your family but your parents?"

"I'm not. But Brett is getting pretty liberal now that he's not living with my aunt and uncle anymore," Jolene explained.

"That's good," Ellie said on her way to her small closet. "I hope you said only nice things about me!"

"There's nothing but good stuff about you!" She heard a rustle from the corner. "What are you doing?"

"I found something for you today when I was walking downtown."

"A present? For Thanksgiving?"

Ellie sat back down in front of the computer. "Sort of. Close your eyes!" Although a Thanksgiving present seemed absurd,

Jolene did as she was told. "Okay, you can look!" she said gleefully.

Jolene opened her eyes. Ellie was smiling brightly with a small rectangular sticker held up below her chin.

"*I heard it on NPR*," Jolene read with a grin.

"Well, I would say about eighty-five percent of the topics you talk about are thanks to NPR. Everything else is from trashy TV shows about adolescence."

Jolene pulled the covers up over her face to hide her reaction.

"I can practically hear you smiling! You know I'm telling the truth!"

Jolene poked her head back out. "You're right. But those TV shows aren't trashy! That descriptor needs to be reserved for that awful MTV show *you* love," she said.

Ellie gasped in mock horror. "How dare you besmirch my show!"

They giggled.

"I love it. I can't wait to stick it on my laptop. Thanks El."

Jolene couldn't believe she had found Ellie after so many years together on the same campus. Every day they spent in each other's company just made her more certain that they were on to something. They were made for each other. It sounded like the most ridiculous sentiment, but in her heart, Jolene knew it was the truth. No one else had ever caused these emotions to surface before. She was a better person with Ellie in her life, and she wasn't afraid to admit it.

"Wanna watch some trashy TV together before bed?"

"I knew there was a reason I liked you," Jolene answered. In truth, the list of reasons grew longer each day; the first would always be Ellie's positivity. She seemed to possess a never-ending supply of happiness, despite problems at home and in her a cappella group, and a perpetual mountain of homework about to bury her. Jolene hoped some of that optimism would transfer to her over time.

"Dibs on picking the show," Ellie interrupted.

"Let me guess, that MTV show has a new episode?"

"Maybe," Ellie trailed off with a wicked grin.

Jolene sighed dramatically, pulling Smiley the stuffed cat close to her chest. "All right, anything for you. I guess I could always mute it and you would never know."

"Oh, I'm going to quiz you on it later," Ellie assured.

"Ugh, all right. I give up," Jolene flopped back against her nest of pillows.

Ellie whooped in joy and settled into her own bed. "You're gonna love it," she promised.

"We'll see," Jolene groaned. If nothing else, she would love spending the rest of the evening curled up in the presence of the only woman who had ever made her feel this way. She would sit through hours of the worst television ever created just to hear Ellie laugh across the spotty Skype connection.

CHAPTER NINETEEN

Could this be more embarrassing?

Ellie covered her face with both hands as Rose continued her interrogation. She had casually mentioned Jolene, which caused Rose to latch on to the topic with fervor usually reserved for students who flooded the café during snow days on campus. The barrage of questions hadn't let up in what felt like hours. Rose's most recent line of questioning strayed into very personal territory. Too personal, if Ellie were being honest. But, she trusted Rose's opinion—even when she trod close to the edge of where good manners went to die.

"Girl!" Rose exclaimed, wielding a knife far too casually.

"Rose!" Ellie whimpered, praying her blush would prove that the topic was too embarrassing for her to address, even in front of friends.

"I need to know these things. I want to make sure this Jo girl is good enough for my best worker," she explained.

"Hey!" Xiaoli grabbed some vegetables off the platter at the kitchen island and shot a skeptical look toward their boss.

"Oh, I only say she's my favorite so she'll tell me all the gossip," Rose explained. "You'll be my favorite when you're a senior and you have good stuff to share with me, don't you worry."

Xiaoli grinned and bit into a carrot. "What's the gossip?" she asked nonchalantly.

Ellie dropped her head to the counter. "It's not gossip if it's about someone in the room who just doesn't feel like sharing every piece of information with her nosy boss."

"Did you just call me bossy?" Rose demanded.

"Nosy! But yes, you are also bossy on the rare occasion. Like now, for example," she groaned.

"Ah, I'm just preparing you for the real world. Think of when you're working at a museum and some bossy lady with a paring knife starts pressuring you for information."

"I don't think that's likely to happen," Xiaoli interjected.

"Hey now! You're not helping. Go set the table or something. Be useful!"

"Ellie's right. You *are* bossy," Xiaoli said over her shoulder.

"And don't forget it!" Rose replied a second after she had left the room.

Ellie risked a glance up from the counter. Rose was staring at her with a no-nonsense look.

"Fine! Yes, we have."

Rose put down the knife before clapping and doing a little dance.

"Ooo baby! You're in deep now! Ooo you love her!" she crooned.

Ellie blushed again and grabbed at the package of Oreos she had brought. The admission that she and Jolene had slept together was just the tip of the iceberg.

"Don't ruin your dinner," Rose chastised.

"I need strength if you're going to keep questioning me about my love life," she explained through a mouthful of chocolate and icing.

Rose hummed thoughtfully. "Okay, so you've talked every night since break started. Have you done the nasty since then?" she questioned.

Ellie almost gagged on the remains of her Oreo.

"No!"

"What? It's nothing to be ashamed of! You miss her. She misses you. You have a little video chat and things get a little naughty. I think we've all been in that predicament before."

"No. Nope, we have not all been in that predicament. We've only been apart for, like, four days!" She cleared her throat and lowered her voice. "And we've only had sex that one time."

Rose sucked in a deep breath. "Well, I predict that the next time it happens will be pretty memorable. '*Always toward absent lovers love's tide stronger flows*' and all that," she recited.

Ellie tried to decipher the strange saying.

"Is that like '*Absence makes the heart grow fonder?*'"

"Yes ma'am. That's exactly what that is like. It's the poet Sextus Propertius explaining that exact concept before people like you started bastardizing it into that little chestnut of a saying," she ranted.

"Your knowledge of obscure poetry is wasted at the café, Rose," Ellie stated.

"It sure is, girl."

"You should give that book of yours another shot."

"What, in all my spare hours? No, no," Rose chided her. "Don't change the subject! We're talking about you today. Back to this Joey of yours."

"I don't think she would approve of being called 'Joey,'" Ellie explained.

"Okay. Your Jojo, then. What's her major?"

"American Studies. Politics and all that."

Rose hummed to herself for a minute. "Does she want to be a politician?" she asked.

"I don't know. I don't think so. She seems more like the backstage campaign-y type of person."

"Just keep in mind that any sex tape you two make would certainly reflect poorly on her future campaign, if she were to have one."

Ellie pinched her temples. "Rose! We're not making a sex tape! We've only been together for, like, two and a half weeks. And we've been in separate states for that half a week." It surprised her to think of how little time she had actually been dating Jolene. In her mind, their relationship seemed to go back to that first day in class together. It was those first few barbs that set them onto this path. Their first date had been in the café over a shared notebook and empty PowerPoint slides. That beatbox tutorial was the first invitation for everything that followed.

"I'm just being your voice of reason." Rose held up her hands in innocence. "These are things that you have to keep in mind."

"Thanks, but I think that's something we'll keep on the back burner for the time being," Ellie said.

"Good." Rose turned back to the fruit she was dicing. "I don't want to see you get hurt. Don't tell the other girls, but you really *are* my favorite."

"Rose!" Xiaoli exclaimed as she threw her hands up in the air and spun on her heel to walk back out of the kitchen.

"Come on! How was I supposed to know you were back in here, Xiaoli? If only you cleaned tables in the café as fast as you set my dinner table!"

Ellie covered her mouth to hide a smile.

"I love you, girl!" Rose yelled at the doorway to the other room.

"Not as much as you love Ellie, clearly!" Xiaoli responded from the living room amidst a cheer from the other café employees.

Rose walked to the doorway. "Fine, to prove my love I won't invite Ellie to Thanksgiving next year," she exclaimed.

"She's a senior! She won't be here next year! Don't try to outsmart me, boss," Xiaoli retorted.

Rose moaned on her way back to the cutting board.

"I can never win with you girls, always hovering around listening to every word I say."

She was so lucky to have Rose. She was a pseudo-sister, mother bear, and voice of reason all rolled into one frizzy-haired package. Ellie's time at Jones University had been difficult, but it was made bearable with Rose's constant support and friendship. She knew that Rose would be in her life, even after she moved away from East Westwick.

"You're the best, Rose. Thanks for looking out for me."

"Anytime girl. You keep me in the loop, you hear?"

"Yes ma'am," she answered.

"What day is Jojo coming back to campus?"

"Saturday afternoon," Ellie said dreamily, her thoughts already stuck on the day they would spend together. She had planned the rest of her break accordingly, positive that she would be useless once she and Jolene were back in the same room.

"Well, don't rush things. You've got plenty of time to let the whole thing just grow naturally. Don't force it," Rose advised.

Nothing felt forced so far, and she didn't expect that to change any time soon.

"I mean, what's the point of the senior slide," Rose continued, "if you're not using it as an excuse to hang out with your hot girlfriend all day and night? Forget classes!"

Ellie rolled her eyes. "Maybe. But you know how I like going to class."

"Yeah, I'm aware. You're a weirdo. But try to give yourself some free time next semester so you can spend it with her. Who knows where you'll be after graduation."

"Yeah," Ellie murmured. That big uncertain question still hung over her future. She didn't know where she would be, but it seemed less foreboding now that she wasn't facing the prospect alone. Maybe she and Jolene would step out into the real world together, hand in hand, with their matching caps and gowns. The thought warmed her from the inside.

"But no skipping your shifts, okay?"

She snapped out of her reverie. "Of course not, boss," she assured.

"Good," Rose replied. She returned to the pot slowly simmering on the stovetop, and left Ellie to think over their conversation. The future was big and uncertain, but she could handle it. Ellie ate another cookie as she pictured the possibilities.

CHAPTER TWENTY

Hurry up, idiots!

Jolene practically snarled as the old couple slowly crossed the intersection. She was back in East Westwick, exactly one tenth of a mile from campus, but it still felt like she had miles left to go. Her GPS arrival time ticked back another minute while she sat impatiently at the traffic light. Jolene wanted to thump her head against the steering wheel because of the delay, which had already been made worse by the fresh snow. The roads were getting more treacherous as the day grew colder and darker.

She was so happy that Thanksgiving break was over and she could spend the remainder of the weekend curled up with Ellie and some of the homework she had neglected while visiting her family. Late-night video chats were great, but they were nothing compared to being next to the warm, beautiful body of her girlfriend. She thought back to their last call. Ellie had serenaded her with a few Christmas carols. Jolene had moaned that Christmas was encroaching on her enjoyment of turkey leftovers and the few remaining crunchy leaves that hid in the corner of her garage. But, in reality, she loved it when Ellie sang just for her. It took her right back to the a cappella jam that had brought them together for the first time after weeks of homework and slyly flirtatious texts. As the traffic light turned green, Jolene shook herself from the emotional pining that seemed to overtake her whenever she thought about Ellie sitting alone in the Quad. She carefully drove the last tenth of a mile to campus and pulled into the snowy parking lot behind her dorm.

She retrieved her duffel bag of clean clothes and Smiley the cat, stuffed into the side pocket of her bag on a whim. As she lifted her laundry out of the backseat, she felt a hard slap on her back. She turned to see Ellie a few yards away, complete with rosy cheeks, pink mittens and a giant scarf covering most of her face. She glanced at Ellie's hands, snowball at the ready.

"Welcome home!" Ellie cheered.

Jolene placed a hand on her hip and frowned dramatically.

"It's good to be back, but I think I'm about to be ambushed."

"Now, who would do that?" Ellie asked innocently as she slowly inched closer to Jolene.

"Whoever just hit me with that snowball," she responded, bending over to drop her duffel bag and form her own ammunition. Ellie's look just grew more devilish.

"I didn't see anyone. You must be imagining things. Too much turkey or something," Ellie replied wickedly.

Jolene pushed her lower lip out to try and get some sympathy. "This isn't going to be a fair fight. I don't have mittens," she whined.

"Oh, you're going to surrender before you get frostbite. Don't worry!"

And with that, Ellie chucked another snowball, which hit Jolene squarely in the chest.

"Hey! Boobs are out of bounds!" Jolene screamed as she threw her own snowball back. They dissolved into laughter as they lobbed the still-fluffy snow at each other. Both girls ran through the thin layer of snow and took cover behind the small piles left behind by the plows from their early morning attempt to clear the lots. Jolene hooted with glee as she hit Ellie in the ear and quickly took the opportunity to pin her girlfriend against the hood of her car.

"No escape now," she teased.

"Maybe I don't want to escape. Stockholm syndrome is setting in," Ellie answered, batting her eyelashes cutely.

"That was fast. I don't think that would—" her explanation of the typical case of Stockholm syndrome was cut off with a warm press of lips against her own. She melted into Ellie's body, happy to be back in the arms of her girlfriend; the cold air around them was no match for the warmth between them. Jolene lowered her lips to a patch of creamy neck not covered by Ellie's scarf. It was tantalizing, but not enough. Never enough. Jolene rubbed her nose along Ellie's jaw, as she slowly edged her way closer to Ellie's lips. It felt magnetic, she realized, as their mouths slotted together again. She heard a muffled sound of pleasure come from the body beneath hers and smiled into their kiss. Ellie's hands were obscured beneath the heavy, snow-soaked mittens, but she could still feel those fingers scrabble for something to hold on to, finally resting at her hips with a tight squeeze. Jolene pulled back at the pressure, at once excited and overwhelmed. She could feel Ellie's quick breath ghost warmly against her throat. After another minute of warm embrace, she pulled back.

"Should we go inside?" she asked, trying to find some control in the words.

"Yeah." Ellie breathed harshly. "I seem to remember you having some hot chocolate somewhere in your room." She picked up the snow-spattered duffel bag sitting by the car.

"You remember correctly."

CHAPTER TWENTY-ONE

What could be better than this?

Ellie rested her hot chocolate on the windowsill, its steam beautiful against the last of the afternoon light that poured through the window, before she burrowed back beneath the duvet. Between the warm sheets, the warm drink, and the warm body, Ellie couldn't imagine a better way to start the second half of the semester. She was optimistic about everything: her schoolwork, her café shifts, the last a cappella performance, and, mostly, the woman stretched out beside her. The breathtaking kiss outside had just proved how good life could be.

"Worrying about homework already?" Jolene whispered into Ellie's ear.

"Not even close. I'm just thinking about how lucky I am right now."

"That's just what I was thinking," Jolene admitted with a quick peck to Ellie's temple.

Ellie warmed at the display of affection and swiveled a bit to admire her girlfriend in profile. She had long since memorized every detail of her face, but there was something novel about seeing her up close again after a week apart. Jolene turned to look at Ellie. They studied each other intently before Ellie hurriedly moved in for a kiss, accidentally bumping their noses together in the process.

"Sorry," she apologized quickly.

Jolene reached up to rub at her nose, slightly numb from the weather. "No need to apologize for that. Any kiss from you is a kiss I enjoy. I'm open to all of them," Jolene joked.

Ellie slid an arm across Jolene's stomach and pulled her closer under the sheets. She buried her face in Jolene's neck, eager to savor the sensation of her again.

"I love you," she said easily, muffled by Jolene's sweater and long hair. She felt her telltale heart grind to a standstill, her face heated as she realized she had just said the three little words without a second thought. She could feel her own body stiffen at the realization of what she had done. She had never said it to anyone before but then, she had never felt like this before either.

"I love you too," Jolene murmured.

Ellie's thoughts quieted as she registered Jolene's words.

"You do?" she asked, poking her head out from the long curtain of hair hiding her eyes from Jolene's.

"Yes."

Ellie's whole body felt like jelly as she let Jolene's calm, assured response sink in. She loved someone and was loved in return. Ellie felt like she could yell out of sheer joy. If she could go back in time and tell her younger self that one day this would be her life, she would do it in a moment. All the years of self-loathing over the realization that she was bisexual floated away, instead replaced by the sensation of a steady heartbeat that pounded against her ear and the warm arms that held her close. If the high school bullies could see her now! Jolene squeezed her around the middle and ran a hand through her locks. Adoringly, Ellie met Jolene's eyes. As Jolene traced careful fingers across her features, Ellie wondered momentarily what she saw that captivated her.

She let the warmth of Jolene's long fingers soak into her skin as they traced the edge of her hairline and then moved to her chin, tracing her bottom lip in smooth strokes before she caught it between her lips. She kissed at her girlfriend's thumb, grazing her teeth along the digit as it slipped further into her mouth. Jolene pulled free and quickly replaced it with her lips and tongue, delving into Ellie's eager mouth. Ellie's breath grew harsh as she tried to keep calm despite the tongue dancing across her sensitive mouth. Jolene's hands slipped around Ellie's waist and gently pushed her onto her back, dislodging the duvet which exposed them to the cool air. Jolene settled her full weight onto Ellie. The clothes between them left little to the imagination as Jolene pressed one thigh into the gap between her legs. Ellie couldn't stop the small roll of her hips at the slight contact, and her teeth caught on the edge of Jolene's lower lip.

When Ellie pulled impatiently at Jolene's shirt, she quickly removed it. Ellie's eyes widened as she realized that her girlfriend was without a bra. Jolene turned to rip Ellie's own shirt off next, and reached under her body to expertly unhook the agitating bra as only another woman could do. She held her breath as Jolene bent down to latch onto one of her exposed nipples, awaiting the spike of pleasure. She was only half undressed and Ellie already felt like she could die of bliss. Ellie guided Jolene up so their lips could meet again and grabbed Jolene's ass. Jolene responded by grinding her pelvis down against Ellie's thigh, hissing into the air shared between them. Ellie felt a shudder run through her as the pressure mounted, but whined when Jolene leaned back, separating them from mouth to chest.

"Are you stopping?" she asked, panting for air.

"Not unless you want me to!" Jolene responded, a wicked glint in her eyes.

"Oh god, don't stop," Ellie begged.

Jolene quickly unzipped Ellie's jeans and licked her long fingers before slipping them into Ellie's panties. She gasped as Jolene pressed their bodies back together. The alignment was perfect for Ellie, her nipples aching as Jolene pushed into the wetness between her legs. Her back arched against the contact, her hips canted as she craved more. She clung desperately into the soft skin of Jolene's hip, a perfect hand-hold as she lost control. She whimpered and tried to focus on kissing Jolene, but was unavoidably distracted by the pleasure of Jolene's fingers against her clit. She cried out, squeezing Jolene's hips, as she gave in to her lover's touch.

Slowly, Ellie opened her eyes as Jolene collapsed next to her and settled her hand on Ellie's sensitive breast.

"I'll pay you back," Ellie panted. "I promise." With her eyes still closed, she could only hear Jolene's breathy laugh, her warm lips against her neck and her body wrapped closer to Ellie's own.

"I missed you, El."

Ellie settled into the afterglow. "I can't believe this is my life," she murmured. Jolene's eyes crinkled with a contented look.

"I find myself thinking the same thing."

"I could just stay here forever."

Jolene hummed. "But I think Rose would be mad if I kept you from work."

"Oh my god, I can't wait to walk in on Monday. She's going to pester me the moment I get there. I think she can sense when people have had important love milestones." Ellie smiled. "Or sex."

"Let me know if you need to be rescued," Jolene offered.

Ellie raised an eyebrow. "I'm not a damsel," she harrumphed.

Jolene pressed a kiss to her neck. "No, you're my knight in shining armor."

"A knight, huh? I could work with that." Ellie paused, still too tired to think properly. "But only if we're both knights and we take turns saving each other occasionally," she countered.

Jolene looked into the distance for a few beats, brow knotted in thought. "That sounds a lot like *Xena: Warrior Princess* to me."

"I would be pretty okay if my life resembled the plot of *Xena*."

Jolene laughed. "You'll need to purchase more leather for your wardrobe."

Ellie worked up the energy to roll on top of Jolene. She pinned her in place and kissed her neck before she collapsed against her, her limbs like jelly.

"I think you have enough leather for the both of us."

"Just the boots!" Jolene griped, her voice muffled against Ellie's skin.

Ellie took the opportunity to tickle Jolene while she was pinned beneath her, squirming and begging for mercy. Once Ellie gave in to the protests, Jolene pushed her off so they were lying side by side. Ellie grabbed the edge of the forgotten duvet and pulled it over their exposed bodies.

"I love you, my little warrior princess" Jolene said, still a little breathless from the tickling.

"Little?" Ellie questioned.

"Well, you *are* shorter than me," Jolene defended.

"Not by that much. Like, maybe three inches!"

When Jolene rolled her eyes, Ellie laughed.

She calmed herself with a deep breath and looked into Jolene's captivating eyes. "I love you too, my slightly taller warrior princess," Ellie whispered.

She tried to memorize the look of pure joy etched on Jolene's face before she kissed her. She didn't think anything could be better than this.

CHAPTER TWENTY-TWO

It's like they're speaking another language.

"I knew they would get on like a house fire," Jolene said to Natalie, taking another fry from Ellie's plate while she was otherwise occupied.

Mo threw her arms out as she launched back into her tirade. Ellie watched with deep concentration, interjecting her own thoughts whenever Mo took a breath or a bite of her veggie burger.

"Who knew a house fire would be so boring for the rest of the table to watch," Natalie deadpanned.

Jolene grinned. Her friends had finally convinced Jolene to share Ellie on one of their date nights and, so far, it seemed like the hassle to get everyone together was worth it. Ellie and Mo easily connected over their shared love of all things school related. Their conversation had quickly turned into an in-depth discussion about the minutiae of academic probation policies.

"El?" Jolene interrupted.

"Yeah?" she asked, turning from Mo, who was about to add another point to her long list of flaws with Jones University's current academic probation system. Jolene and Natalie had both heard the list many times, usually after one of Mo's long Honor Board hearings. She guessed that Mo would keep talking all night if they let her.

"Natalie wants to meet you too," she offered, pointing to the redhead seated across from her.

"Feeling jealous?" Mo nudged at Natalie's ribs.

"No, just bored by you droning on. The usual, really," she explained.

The group laughed as Ellie refocused on Natalie.

"Sorry. Guess I got wrapped up in the debate," she apologized.

"Seems like you'll fit right in here," Natalie said with a shrug. "Jo loves dinner debates too."

"That is true. It's either that or a cappella gossip. That's the range of topics I can manage," Jolene agreed.

"Ah yes, the ever present a cappella gossip," Natalie moaned.

"You're in the Jones Tones, right Ellie?" Mo asked between bites.

"Yeah. I'm their treasurer."

"Sounds like a lot of work," Mo observed.

"It can be, but being the treasurer isn't too hard. It's not like we're spending buckets of money each week," she continued. "We really only have two events each semester that require a bit of spending. Everything else is just collecting payment after we perform at socials and stuff."

"Do you write any of the arrangements?" Natalie asked.

"Not usually. We mostly leave that to our president, Sylvia. She's a genius when it comes to the music side of things. But I've been working on one for a few weeks, just for fun. It needs a lot of work though," she said.

"Please tell me it will require someone to rap. Those are always my favorites. Nicki Minaj?" Mo practically begged.

Ellie grimaced. "Sorry, no. It's a mash-up of a Passenger and Bastille song."

"I didn't know you were working on that," Jolene interjected. It sounded like a good idea, depending on the songs she had picked. Current hits were always pretty well liked by the audiences at Jones. Usually, the groups on campus fought over who could sing them. Jolene had witnessed her fair share of squabbles between rival groups, especially when it came to new songs from artists everyone loved.

"Yeah, I had them on a playlist back to back and it occurred to me that they would work really well together," Ellie explained.

"That sounds really interesting. When can we hear it?" Natalie asked.

"Well, I'd have to finish it first. But, probably at our final jam in the spring. I hope you'll all come see it," she answered enthusiastically, looking between the three of them.

Jolene caught Natalie's scrutiny from across the table but shook it off, unsure of why Natalie was staring her down. She focused on Ellie.

"Let me know if you need any help with the arrangement. I'm a masterful coach when it comes to a cappella. I'm sure I have one student who would recommend me," Jolene said playfully.

"Ew. Stop! It's too cute," Mo whined.

Jolene saw Ellie's face heat and squeezed her hand under the table.

"I'm getting cake," Natalie said as she stood up. "Jo, come get a piece for your long-suffering girlfriend." She signaled toward the dessert station in the corner.

Jolene followed Natalie but, once they arrived at the dessert table, knew that she was in trouble.

"Does Ellie know you're a January grad?"

Jolene felt herself deflate.

"No."

Natalie looked over at the table. Mo and Ellie spoke together animatedly—probably already back to their discussion about academics. She turned back to Jolene and looked at her sympathetically while Jolene's stomach dropped like a lead weight.

"You need to be careful, Jo. You could end up hurting a lot of people if you don't tell her the truth," she warned.

"Yeah."

"Yeah," Natalie replied seriously. "Just think about what you're doing." She picked up her cake and walked back to the table. Jolene stood, rooted to the spot, and watched Ellie's convivial interaction with her friends. Hurting Ellie was the last thing she wanted to do but she didn't know how to bring up her early graduation without doing just that. The longer she waited the harder it got, and now she found herself between a rock and a hard place. Finals were just around the corner, so to tell her now could just make it worse. Maybe she could wait until after Ellie was done with finals. They would have all the time they needed to discuss it once winter break started. She picked up two pieces of cake and headed back to the table. It could wait another two weeks.

"You're back in time to hear the latest Honor Board gossip," Ellie said as Jolene placed the cake in front of her.

"Really?"

Mo sobered. "Well, I'm not technically allowed to reveal anything from our investigations. So, you're not hearing this from me." She looked at everyone to make sure they understood before she continued.

"Go on," Natalie prodded, stabbing her fork into the hardened icing on her plate.

"We've just had three separate cases come to the board with people cheating on term papers," she started. "And not in the Wikipedia way either. That's old hat, I guess. The new thing, apparently, is to bump up word counts in papers submitted through the online system. Students are adding a row or two of gibberish to the end of every paragraph and then changing the font color to white. It's invisible to the grader, but it can increase the word count by a couple hundred to meet the quota." Mo was wide-eyed, waiting for a response from the group.

"Wow," Natalie said.

"I know!" Mo bowed her head. "It's unbelievable."

"I wish I had thought of it," Natalie mused.

Mo swatted at Natalie's arm and accused her of being a bad influence. Ellie rubbed Jolene's back, clearly caught up in the exchange. Jolene's anxiety felt like it was going to burst through her rib-cage, and she had an inkling that, from now on, every one of Ellie's smiles would produce a razor-sharp spike of guilt. She swallowed, hoping that she was right about her decision: that it could, in fact, wait another two weeks.

CHAPTER TWENTY-THREE

It just won't fit.

Ellie scrunched up another piece of paper. She had been trying to figure out her course schedule for the past hour, but couldn't make it all work. She had three credits remaining to complete her Museum Studies major and another to complete her Study of Women and Gender minor. That would be the normal course load, but there were at least three other classes that she still wanted to take before graduation. Her shoulders tightened with frustration, realizing that this would be her last opportunity to study some of these subjects. Grad school probably wouldn't offer courses like 'History 321: Nostalgia in Context' or 'Art History 281: Wanderlust.' A knock on the door startled her and Jolene poked her head around the corner.

"Hey you!" Jolene greeted brightly, her cheeks slightly pink from the wintery wind.

Ellie leaned back and rubbed at her face. "Jeez you're a sight for sore eyes."

Jolene sat on the bed. "Homework?" she asked.

Ellie wanted to sprawl across the small bed with Jolene and cuddle for hours, but knew they both had to be at a cappella rehearsals after dinner and there was always some homework to be done.

"No. I've been trying to figure out my class schedule for next semester, but I can't decide. I don't want to overload on classes because then I'll miss out on senior stuff, but I don't want to take only what's required because there are so many classes that sound amazing." Jolene nodded. "What's your schedule going to be like?" Ellie asked, putting on her shoes so they could head downstairs to the dining hall. Tonight was their weekly date night in the Quad and she really hoped the dining staff had chosen something better than last week's sloppy ravioli. Her simple question was met with a steady silence.

"What?" She glanced at Jolene.

The only answer was Jolene's panicked expression.

"What's wrong?" Ellie asked.

"El, I'm a J grad," Jolene said quietly.

Ellie's thoughts evaporated. She felt herself stop breathing as her heart began to pound against her ribs. That couldn't be right. If Jolene were really a J grad it meant they only had two weeks left together. Jolene would move off campus and she'd be alone at Jones. For good. And one of those weeks would be filled with reading period and exams. Her mind raced.

"I don't understand."

Jolene exhaled, pain clear in her eyes.

"I'm graduating a semester early so I can get out in the political world as soon as possible. I'm waiting to hear back from a few campaigns to see if they want me, but I think I'll be moving home after the semester ends."

"Home? With your parents in New Hampshire?"

Jolene sighed again, her eyes focused on the floor. "No. New Mexico," she mumbled.

Ellie thought back to the long nights they had stayed up talking over fall break. Jolene had insisted that New Hampshire never really felt like home and that holidays in the foreign house seemed different than the ones that had been spent in her childhood home. She had never felt settled in New Hampshire, she claimed, and still considered New Mexico home. It was where Jolene's grandparents still lived, where she had attended high school, and where she had worked on local campaigns over the past few summers. Ellie's thoughts stuttered again. New Mexico was over two thousand miles away from Jones University.

She felt her heart break. "You're moving across the country in two weeks and you're just telling me now?" she asked.

"I guess—"

"You *guess*?" Ellie interrupted. "How could you not tell me this?"

"I don't know!" Jolene cried.

"Why wasn't this one of the first things you told me?"

"It was never a good time, El," she said.

"And now *is*?" Ellie asked, her voice thick with tears. Now was definitely not a good time. She couldn't fathom Jolene's thought process.

Jolene looked desperate. "I didn't want to spoil what we have!"

"And you didn't think putting it off would spoil it?" Ellie demanded.

"Hold on."

"No! I don't know what you were thinking! Was this just an easy thing for you? To swoop into my life for a few months and then leave me in the dust while you start a new life?"

"I'm not leaving you," Jolene spluttered.

Ellie's eyes filled with tears. "Well, it sure *seems* like it," she snapped. "You're going back to New Mexico!"

"That doesn't mean we can't still be together," Jolene pleaded.

"Why would you stay with me when there are plenty of people back home that love you?" Ellie demanded.

Jolene looked stunned. "Please Ellie. You know I'm over her."

"Her" was Jolene's high school sweetheart and the first person to whom Jolene had said *I love you*. Ever since Jolene had described her, Ellie had felt insecure, even though Jolene insisted that her feelings for her ex had passed. She gathered her strength and pressed on.

"I need you to leave me alone right now," Ellie announced.

"Ellie," Jolene begged, "please, let's talk about this. I don't want to lose you."

Ellie's eyes burned. She wanted to throw Jolene out of the room before the tears fell. They had only been a couple for a little over a month but she knew that she was madly in love with Jolene. But, that fact didn't change the lie: Jolene had kept her plans a secret. She had told Ellie she loved her and yet withheld vital information. On top of that, at the busiest and most difficult time of the semester, she had to deal with both her emotions *and* her finals. Jolene would leave Ellie behind and walk right back into the open arms of a woman who apparently loved Jolene as much as she did. She and Jolene would be two thousand miles apart while Jolene and her ex would essentially be neighbors. How could she compete with that?

"Too late. Get out," she said calmly, pointing at the door.

"What are you saying?"

Ellie noted the lack of emotion on Jolene's face but knew that her own eyes were shiny with the unshed tears. Jolene looked as composed as ever—a cool girl to the core. She knew that the nagging feeling in the back of her mind since the beginning of their relationship had been right all along: she wasn't enough. Ellie was getting dumped by the most wonderful woman she had ever known and in the most nonchalant way imaginable. Jolene had let time do the dirty work for her. It was all a game and Ellie had just lost the final round.

"I'm saying we're done. Please leave me alone."

Ellie turned her back to Jolene. Through tears, she trained her eyes on the course guide still open on her laptop until she heard the sound of Jolene's heavy boots fade down the hallway. Ellie took a deep breath, struggling to keep her composure, but a tear slipped down her cheek. With a shaky hand, she slammed the computer shut and then the door. A cappella rehearsal would have to wait for another day; there was no way she could leave her room tonight after Jolene had broken her heart so effortlessly.

CHAPTER TWENTY-FOUR

Thank god it's over.

Jolene packed her final box into the car. She snapped the trunk closed and leaned her hip against the cold metal. The snow had melted, which had left only soggy brown grass and barren trees around campus. She could see Ellie's dorm in the distance through the line of trees at the far edge of the parking lot. She looked down at her boots, trying to think of anything else she had forgotten in Buchman Hall.

The past two weeks had been terrible. She had texted Ellie furiously at first, unsuccessfully trying to make her listen to reason. But as the silence stretched on, she realized her mistake had truly devastated Ellie and that her reasons meant nothing from Ellie's point of view. She tearfully turned to Mo and Natalie and asked for help. They had dropped everything to comfort her. Mo went to the café, hoping that her instant rapport with Ellie would allow her the opportunity to talk with her and, maybe, plead Jolene's case. But Mo had returned unsuccessful from her many trips across campus. Ellie was never there.

That news worried Jolene the most. She knew Ellie needed the money and that she was an essential staff member at the café. Even during finals, she would have picked up some extra shifts. Jolene had paced through the Quad that evening, trying to clear her head, but also hoping to glimpse Ellie. She had picked out her window, but the light was off. Jolene's heart had lurched in her chest.

She finally caught sight of Ellie one afternoon during finals as they passed in a busy hallway, moving quickly toward a lecture hall with her head buried in a textbook as she crammed until the last possible second. Jolene missed her deeply, and yearned to reach out but still felt like there was nothing to be done now. She had been careless and overlooked how her early graduation would affect Ellie. A million excuses ran through her thoughts whenever she remembered their last conversation. She could have explained her reasoning: that talking about it before finals would only hurt both of their grades. Or that by the time they began dating it had been too late to bring it up naturally. She should have explained that they had all of winter break to talk about their possible future together, and that her past relationships meant nothing to her anymore. It was too late for all of that now though. The future she once dreamed of had evaporated the moment Ellie asked her to leave that night. Jolene knew that she could spend hours explaining herself, but it wouldn't make a difference now. She had lost Ellie's trust and now she was gone.

Jolene got into her car and rested her head on the steering wheel to pull herself together. The drive from East Westwick back to her grandparents' house in New Mexico would take three days if she pushed herself. And she was going to push herself. There was no reason not to. She took out her phone to select a podcast, but stopped as her thumb hovered over the message app. She opened it and scrolled up through her many woeful attempts to explain things and looked at the last text she had received from Ellie on that horrible night.

Regular dinner date at 5:30? :)

She blinked back the tears and tapped a final text to Ellie before she had time to change her mind. She had to say something else, and was determined that their last words should not determine their future. Even if she never saw Ellie again, she wanted to make it clear that her own carelessness had cost her the greatest thing in her life. She had gambled with Ellie's affection and dashed their future to pieces.

I should say that I hope your finals went well, but I know that they did because you're the best student I've ever met. Instead, I'll say I hope you can forgive me one day because that's something I'm not so sure about. I'm sorry, Ellie.

For five interminable minutes, she waited for a response. When nothing came, she pulled out of the parking lot with a heavy heart, and headed for New Mexico.

CHAPTER TWENTY-FIVE

Get it together.

Ellie breathed deeply in an attempt to calm the tears. She felt Rose's large hand grip her shoulder tightly.

"I'm sorry, girl. This sucks."

Ellie threw her phone onto Rose's desk and grabbed a tissue from the box. Rose sat down in the chair beside her and continued to pat Ellie's knee. Her sniffles sounded loud in the cramped office.

As soon as Ellie saw Jolene's text she had run to the café, sure that Rose would know what to do about it. Some small part of her wanted to reply—to run to the parking lot and hear that Jolene hadn't meant to hurt her, that it was all a silly mistake, and to accept her apology. Ellie's tears ebbed as she justified her impulse, but Rose had a different opinion about the situation.

"I know it's hard. But one text isn't an apology. She needs to be standing in front of you or, better yet, groveling at your feet. Then you could see if she really means it," Rose explained calmly.

"But, how can she apologize if I don't give her the chance?" Ellie asked between breaths.

"She had a bunch of chances, baby. She's had two whole weeks of chances."

"But, finals—"

"Yeah, your finals, which she almost derailed because of her stupid lie of omission," Rose snarled.

Ellie's tears started up again.

"I'm sorry." She handed Ellie another tissue.

"No, you're right. But how did she think it would end? It seems like the easy way out," Ellie admitted. "Like she wanted to break things off, but was going to wait until she went home for winter break to make it easier."

"Maybe. I bet she just got carried away. I think you both probably did," Rose said with a shrug. "It's easy to forget the important stuff when you're having fun and still in the honeymoon period. Conversation is always the key."

Ellie growled at herself before she blotted at the tears again.

"All right. That's enough! Rose, you have to make sure I don't dwell on this. I need to enjoy my last semester of senior year. Can you do that?"

"Oh yeah, girl. I got this," Rose said with a devilish smirk.

Ellie felt her resolve crumble a bit from Rose's generous support, and pressed her face into the warmth of Rose's broad shoulder.

"Thanks boss."

"Anytime girl," she replied as she hugged Ellie a little too tightly.

Ellie grabbed her phone off Rose's desk. "Okay. I've gotta go pack some stuff before I leave," she explained.

"Feel free to come back early if you need to. My door is always open for you."

Ellie murmured her thanks. "I'll let you know if I need to take you up on that."

Rose turned serious.

"Do you want me to delete her contact info from your phone before you go?"

Ellie looked down at the phone in her hands and felt her grip tighten. There were a lot of sappy texts and photos from their date nights that she should probably delete. Still, she wasn't ready for that yet. She swallowed and put on a brave face.

"Nah. It'll give me something to do when I get home."

Rose pulled Ellie into another tight hug and whispered into her ear. "I can make her regret the day she ever hurt you. Just say the word."

Ellie snorted and thanked Rose again on her way out of the office. She hesitated by the counter and contemplated a milkshake but when she saw Xiaoli's sympathetic look Ellie just walked away. A milkshake wouldn't help her forget.

CHAPTER TWENTY-SIX

Elections suck.

Jolene dropped her shoulder bag onto the lumpy couch in her small apartment and slumped down beside it. Exhausted, she pondered the merits of collapsing onto the cushions for the rest of the night. She had spent the entire day as a volunteer at the Albuquerque School Board elections and she never wanted to do it again. The only people who seemed to turn up for school board elections during the first week of February were retirees who couldn't read the ballot without assistance and the overly aggressive fans of political in-fighting and smack talk. At least she could add it to her résumé. She tried not to think about the complete lack of paid political jobs currently listed on it.

Jolene had been a graduate of Jones University for over a month, but still hadn't secured a full-time job. Luckily, her grandparents let her work in their secondhand bookstore at night and on weekends. Her income was enough for a shabby apartment, but she was far from happy about her situation. For so long she had dreamt of graduating early to get ahead of her peers, but in reality she was just another fish out of water.

Jolene looked at her phone and realized she was due at the bookstore in ten minutes. She swore under her breath and levered herself off the couch, instantly regretting the loss of a comfortable seat. She threw together a peanut butter sandwich and dug her favorite jeans out of the laundry basket in her closet. She had one leg on as her phone rang.

"Hey Gran," she answered as she shimmied into the other leg.

"Hi honey!" her grandmother's voice boomed.

"I might be a few minutes late tonight. The polls just closed," she explained.

"Oh, don't worry. We didn't expect you to come by tonight. We were going to close early and go to Leo's for some pasta instead. Did you want to join us?"

Jolene flopped down onto her couch again. "You and Grandpa should have a date night. Are you sure you don't want me to come in? I don't mind," she lied.

"No, no. You need a rest, honey. Why don't you turn on that show you love and go to bed early? We'll see you tomorrow instead."

"Thanks Gran. I really appreciate it," she said wearily.

"No problem. Have a good night! I can't wait to read all about the results in the paper tomorrow!"

Jolene rolled her eyes. Her gran had no opinion or interest in the school board. She wished her a good night out and hung up. Jolene couldn't help her small shimmy of a dance, despite still being flopped down across the couch. Shifts at the bookstore and an intensive job search had left her with almost no free time. Her first decision was to splurge on a pizza. She ordered online and then looked through the long list of TV shows she wanted to see. She saw lots of reviews for a midseason finale of Ellie's favorite MTV show, felt a pang of remorse, clicked away from the tab and decided to turn on an old election-themed episode of *The West Wing* instead, since that was always her go-to comfort show. Curled up in flannel pajamas, Jolene made a cocoon of blankets on her couch while she waited for her pizza to arrive. One episode turned into three, and a full box of pizza turned into two leftover pieces for breakfast.

As the third episode ended, she opened up a tab for the trashy MTV show again. Jolene pressed play and leaned back, immediately consumed with thoughts of Ellie's passion for these characters. She let her imagination run wild, wondering if Ellie still watched the show or if Jolene had permanently ruined it for her. This unanswered question opened the door to a whole different array of thoughts.

Would she ever see Ellie again to get the chance to apologize? How was Ellie doing? Had she taken on too many classes? Was she swamped with work and café shifts? Did she have a shoulder to cry on? Was she happy again?

Jolene closed her eyes and tried to quiet her thoughts. She didn't know the answer to any of those questions, so what was the point in worrying about it? Jolene had lied to Ellie and let them develop an attachment despite the fact that she knew she would be leaving campus. She had purposely not discussed it with Ellie. Maybe they could have somehow worked it out, but that was another life. There was no one to blame for her current situation and heartache but herself.

She got up from the couch and stumbled into her bedroom, without bothering to turn on the radio. Her first night off had been a real disaster of thoughts that spiraled out of control and emotions she didn't want to address quite yet. She hugged her stuffed cat, Smiley, close to her chest, closed her eyes, and hoped that sleep would come soon so she could stop picturing Ellie's tear-filled eyes and flushed cheeks, as she demanded that Jolene leave her alone. Her own tears slipped sideways off her face and left patterns on her pillow as the lonely minutes ticked by. Jolene missed college. She missed Ellie.

CHAPTER TWENTY-SEVEN

Sylvia's ass looks great in those leggings.

Ellie snapped out of her thoughts as the president of the Jones Tones ordered her sheet music.

"Good practice today, yeah?" Sylvia asked.

Ellie nodded distractedly and turned away from the lanky girl across from her in the empty semicircle of chairs left scattered around the room. Practices had been good lately, mostly because Alyssa had finally, and not unexpectedly, thrown in the towel—both with a cappella and with Sylvia. The on-again, off-again relationship that had been tearing the Jones Tones apart was finally behind them all. If campus gossip was accurate, Alyssa and Sylvia had parted ways over winter break. After so long in the eye of the storm, it felt bizarre to be out of the loop now. Ellie had no idea what the final straw had been, but then again, didn't care. Auditions had secured her replacement almost immediately. The new sophomore was already settled in and, more importantly, pulled her weight at rehearsals. The group dynamics were dramatically improved which eased many of Ellie's worries about the future of the Jones Tones. But Sylvia was still a messy president and Ellie continued to feel the extra weight on her shoulders to make sure the group succeeded.

Her gaze skirted to Sylvia, and she wondered for a moment if Sylvia felt as gutted about losing Alyssa as Ellie did about Jolene. She wasn't so sure. Her pale skin, nose ring and perfectly styled looks only added to her bad girl image that exuded indifference. Ellie had to admit she was a great-looking girl, despite the disagreeable attitude. She shook herself from those thoughts and packed her speakers into her bag.

"You've been quiet lately, El. What's up?" Sylvia asked, her voice suddenly much closer than before. Sylvia stood next to her, one hip against the back of a nearby chair.

"I'm fine," she answered quietly. She didn't think Sylvia wanted to hear about her romantic troubles. The other girl had enough for the both of them. When Sylvia ran her perfectly painted fingernails through her shocking turquoise hair, the undercut hidden beneath the long locks was revealed.

"It doesn't seem like you're fine. This is senior year, kid! You're supposed to be worry free and all that shit."

Ellie wanted to laugh. She was as far from "worry free" as humanly possible. She had signed up for six classes, two more than she needed to graduate, and had picked up extra shifts at the café to save up for her future apartment. Together with the busy a cappella rehearsal schedule, she had no free time. She liked it that way. The less time she had to think about Jolene, the better.

"Just trying to get over an ex." She prayed that Sylvia would understand and let it go.

"Oh yeah, rough stuff, dude," she said. "Was it that chick from Acapellago?"

Ellie swallowed. "Yes." This was getting into dangerous "feelings" territory. She stood to leave but Sylvia spoke before she could make it to the door.

"You're too good for her anyway," she said with a wry grin.

Ellie couldn't tell if Sylvia was serious. She looked back over her shoulder, unable to read Sylvia's body language. She felt her eyes drift down, tracking across the long lines and smooth angles as the other girl made her way toward the exit.

"Thanks," she offered dryly as Sylvia passed.

Sylvia stopped with the door propped halfway open and lifted Ellie's chin with two cool fingers.

"Let me know if you need a pick-me-up fuck."

Ellie's eyes widened as Sylvia slipped out the door. She stood in the doorway as she heard the footsteps echo down the stairwell. Sylvia had a reputation as a bit of a player, but she had no idea she would offer herself so freely. She had heard plenty of stories about Sylvia's various sexual exploits over the years, but Ellie had always assumed that it was a bit of a façade. She suddenly remembered the Halloween party the Jones Tones performed at in the fall of her junior year. An image stuck in her mind of the sexy cowgirl costume Sylvia had worn, especially the skirt that fell tantalizingly low across her hips and the top that left little to imagination. Ellie felt her cheeks heat, instantly regretful. She didn't want those unsavory thoughts. She was still trying to unspool Sylvia's invitation as she slowly made her way down the stairs and into the cool night air, already laced with hints of spring. She decided that nothing could make her get over Jolene, not even sex with Sylvia. If she had learned anything from Alyssa, it was that the smartest decision was to stay away.

CHAPTER TWENTY-EIGHT

L.M.N.O.P

Jolene placed the battered slice of a book by P.K. Page on the shelf next to a few of Lynda Page's more substantial tomes. She casually wondered if they were related and made a mental note to look it up when she got back to a place with cell phone service. She broke down the now-empty cardboard box, scrunched it behind the trashcan, and then perched herself on the threadbare stool behind the register. Two customers milled around slowly and she wondered about their lives. Maybe they would both reach for the same copy of *Wuthering Heights* and then insist that the other take it. Jolene imagined herself suggesting that they share it over coffee, which would cause the goofy-looking boy to stammer and the girl to giggle. Her imagined "meet-cute" fell apart when the boy leaned down to peruse a copy of *Fight Club* and the girl walked out without a second glance.

Jolene sighed and closed her eyes. She was startled when a hand poked at her ribs.

"Sorry honey!" Gran apologized. "Didn't mean to scare you."

Jolene shrugged as her heart rate returned to normal. "Are you heading out for the night?" she asked.

"Yes, if your grandfather would ever stop messing around with that squeaky drawer in the back room."

"Gran, he needs something to keep him out of trouble," Jolene joked.

"Oh, he'll be in trouble if he doesn't shake a leg. It's past my dinnertime!" she boomed.

She knew that no matter how many customers Gran disturbed with her loud voice, her absentminded husband still wouldn't hear a thing. Gran rolled her eyes and squeezed Jolene against her chest, nearly causing her to fall off the stool.

"What are you reading now?" she asked, peering at the book resting against the register.

"Wollstonecraft."

Gran nodded. "Good choice, honey. Just remember, no folding the pages."

"I know," she answered as her grandfather toddled out from the back room. Gran rounded the counter to surreptitiously stand beside him, and offered an arm for support. It was a sight to see, her youthful grandmother beside her grandfather, who seemed to slip through their fingers more and more each day. His hair, once black like her own, was now completely white and frazzled. His glasses seemed to be permanently smudged or lost and his balance was progressively worsening. Still, he refused to use a cane. Gran seemed to take it in stride.

Jolene remembered hot summers spent in this store. She had watched as her grandparents moved around the place like dancers, their movements like magic to her young eyes. She marveled at the way her grandmother, easily the tallest person in her family, could shelve books without a stepstool, and the way her grandfather calculated totals and taxes without using a pen and paper. She remembered sticking out her tongue when they paused their complicated dance around the shop for a quick kiss. Time had certainly changed things.

"Ready for dinner, honey?" Gran asked.

"Hm? Yes, dinner!" her hunched Grandpa answered.

"Don't forget about folding the pages," Gran called over her shoulder.

"Never fold pages! The books will lose their value." Grandpa pushed his glasses back up the bridge of his nose.

Jolene quickly hopped off the stool and ran around a stack of books to beat them to the front of the store. She opened the glass door and the small bell tinkled overhead as she ushered them out.

Jolene kissed them each on the cheek. "Have a good dinner."

She watched as her grandparents made their way to Leo's, the only restaurant Grandpa would patronize now. She exhaled deeply when they made it to the door nearly three minutes later, despite it only being a few doors down. Grandpa opened the door for Gran; his forgetfulness had yet to affect his devotion to his wife of forty-three years. His chivalry was still intact through it all. Jolene hoped she would find someone to care for her like that one day. The goofy-looking boy dinged the concierge bell next to the register, which interrupted the silent prayer for her future. She made her way back to the counter and put aside thoughts of love for another day.

CHAPTER TWENTY-NINE

Why are you doing this?

Ellie looked at her fist in horror. But before she could formulate an alternative plan, the door opened and Sylvia's aquiline face poked out.

"Hey El."

Ellie paused, still completely unsure of herself and why she had come to see Sylvia.

"Can I help you with something?" Sylvia asked as she opened the door to her dorm room even wider. Ellie looked down; the sight of Sylvia made her exponentially more nervous. Sylvia was dressed in a black crop top that clung to her curves, and silver bike shorts that hugged her narrow hips.

"I, uh," was all she could get out.

"Do you want to come in?" Sylvia purred as she moved out of the way, somehow oblivious to Ellie's hesitation.

Ellie shuffled into the stark dorm room whose atmosphere only made her more uncomfortable. The windowsill was covered with shot glasses and wine bottles stuffed with partially burnt candles of different colors. A fire hazard, she thought distantly. Candles weren't allowed in the dorms.

Sylvia lay down on the bed. "You look nervous."

Ellie *was* nervous. She had nothing in common with Sylvia except a cappella and their recent breakups. But even after a week, she hadn't been able to get Sylvia's crude proposition out of her head. Since then, they had seen each other at two rehearsals and Sylvia had yet to mention it again. Ellie wondered if she was just desperate for affection but, for some reason, she felt like she needed this. Whatever "this" meant.

"I am," she answered, trying to keep the nerves out of her voice.

Sylvia's eyebrow arched. "I make you nervous?"

"A little."

Sylvia laughed but Ellie didn't see what was so funny.

"Come sit down."

Ellie did, but left as much space between them on the twin bed as she could.

"I won't bite." Sylvia's look turned wicked. "Unless you want me to."

Ellie shot up from the bed and headed for the door, certain that this was the worst mistake she could make. It had been three months since she had had her heart broken by Jolene, who she was sure would always be her first love. There was a time when she thought Jolene would be her last love too.

Sylvia followed her. "Hey, calm down, El."

Ellie's hand was wrapped around the cold door handle when she felt Sylvia's fingers brush her shoulder.

"We don't have to do anything you don't want to." That purr laced each word.

"I don't know why I'm here," Ellie admitted as she dropped her head to rest against the door. The wood made a dull thud, reminding her that the hallway was inches away and she could leave if she really wanted to.

"I'll make you forget all about her," Sylvia teased.

That sounded like exactly what Ellie needed. Or wanted. She had tried to forget about Jolene—her cool attitude covering up for the nerdy politic beneath, the long hair and stubby fingernails that once loved to trace along the short hair on the nape of Ellie's neck, the kind eyes and even kinder words. She wanted to forget the heartbreak and the love that was still trapped in some small part of her for the girl that had left her. So far, nothing had been able to stop the memories or the heartache.

She released her grip on the door handle. "Okay." Sylvia took her hand and led her back to the bed. Ellie took a deep breath to calm herself but her exhale was interrupted by Sylvia's lips on her own. She closed her eyes, hoping the sensation would wipe away her memories. Sylvia was all teeth and had fingers that explored eagerly. Ellie let herself float, her body warm and responsive to Sylvia's touch. But when an image of Jolene flashed into her mind, tears threatened. She was wrapped in the arms of a near stranger and it wasn't what she wanted after all.

She pushed Sylvia away. "I have to go."

"I'll be right here if you change your mind." Sylvia's saccharine, mocking challenge haunted Ellie as she rushed out the door.

CHAPTER THIRTY

Goddamn it.

Jolene rubbed at her eyes as she rolled over. Her phone's shrill ring was the last thing she wanted to hear.

"Hello?"

"Hey Jojo."

"Dad?" she asked groggily.

"That's me," he said happily.

Jolene could only grump at him at this early hour. "Don't they have time zones on the East Coast?" she asked.

"Indeed they do."

"Why are you calling me so early?" she complained.

"I have some good news." He paused for effect. "Are you sitting down?"

"I'm still in bed, Dad."

"Senator Strelkoff died!"

"What! Why are you happy?" Jolene asked, palming her forehead. "That's awful. You're awful!"

She heard a laugh through the phone. "Well, he was ancient. He might be in a better place now. I certainly hope the afterlife is better than the US Senate."

"Dad," she begged, "what's your point?"

"Well, as you should be aware, after a senator dies in Vermont there's a special election," her dad practically shouted.

"So?"

"So! I happen to know of someone who lives in that lovely neighboring state of ours who is looking for a fresh-faced campaign worker," he explained.

Jolene sat up, fully awake now, hoping against hope that this could be her big break. "What are you saying?" she asked.

"Do you want a job on the campaign?"

"Yes!" she screamed with a fist in the air.

"Calm down, kiddo!"

Jolene couldn't help herself. She got out from under the covers and jumped for joy. A job on a US Senate campaign was exactly the first step she wanted to take. After three months of cold calls and sending résumés filled with only meager internships and volunteer opportunities, she would finally make her first foray into a major political campaign.

"I can't calm down, Dad. I'm so excited!"

He laughed again. "I'm very happy for you, Jojo."

"When do I start?" she asked, running to her laptop to open her calendar.

"As soon as possible. My friend down at the Public Works office here put me in contact with the campaign manager. I talked you up big-time, so you owe me some doughnuts or something," he explained.

"You're the best, Dad."

"Just don't leave your grandparents in the lurch. Make sure you find someone to take over for you at the shop."

She could feel a lecture headed her way. "Of course. There are plenty of penniless college kids in town looking for some extra work. I'll make it happen."

"All right," he murmured.

"Thank you Dad.

"Anything for you, kiddo. I'll send you the campaign manager's info. Make sure you send him an email to follow up and discuss your arrival."

"Don't worry! There's no way I'm letting this one slip through my fingers."

"Good. Now go back to your beauty sleep."

She snorted, barely able to contain her excitement. "How can I sleep now! I've got so much to do! Packing and apartment hunting! Ah! So much planning!"

"I'm sure there are plenty of podcasts to listen to while you do all that boring junk. Tell us when you plan to travel."

"Will do."

"Give your grandparents kisses from us," he continued.

"I'll do that too," she said fondly.

"Love you, Jojo."

"Love you, Dad."

Jolene disconnected the call and ran into the living room to turn on an episode of *The West Wing*. She notched the volume up entirely too loud for the theme song as she hummed along. After that was out of her system, she grabbed a notepad and began to write down her very long to-do list.

CHAPTER THIRTY-ONE

That's not a reassuring look.

"What's up?" Ellie asked.

Her boss cocked her eyebrow, one hand rested on a hip.

"What's up? Oh, you know what's up," Rose answered cryptically.

"I do?"

"Yes," she said as she moved toward the coffee dispenser on the other counter.

Ellie looked around for some hint, but all she saw were the normal weekend customers peppered throughout the café.

"I have no idea what you're getting at, Rose."

"Girl, I'm talking about your complete attitude change," Rose offered through longs sips.

That caught Ellie off guard. She thought she was pretty normal. She explained as much to Rose, but was met with a disbelieving look.

"This time last year you were going on and on about the good weather and all the upcoming exhibitions at MoMa and all that stuff. Nowadays I can barely get a word out of you." Rose frowned.

Ellie knew that Rose was right. Things had changed. She hadn't felt like herself since the breakup. And it was worse now that she was fooling around with Sylvia. She had gone back to Sylvia after her first attempt at a rebound failed. It was far from perfect, but it distracted her from thoughts of Jolene. She picked up a dishtowel and wiped the counter to give herself a reason to look away from Rose's searching glare.

"I think you might be right," she admitted.

"I know I'm right. I've been your boss and—I think we can admit this now—your friend, for four years. You've never been this quiet, even during that time campus lost power for three days!"

Ellie didn't respond to the small attempt at humor.

"Tell me what's running through that head of yours," Rose said.

Ellie weighed her options. Her friends hadn't been much help since returning for their last semester. Everyone was too excited about graduation and finishing thesis assignments on time. And her few a cappella friends wouldn't want to hear about her drama since they had plenty of their own to worry about. Not to mention that conversations about Sylvia could lead to lots of trouble.

"I made a big mistake," she began.

Rose listened silently.

"I tried the rebound thing," she continued, "with the president of my a cappella group."

"And how did that turn out?" Rose sipped her coffee.

Ellie looked back down at the now spotless counter. "It's kind of still going on," she admitted.

Her boss hummed but she sped on before Rose could say anything. "We've hooked up a few times over the past month. Enough times that I think we might technically be dating. I'm not sure. We haven't talked about it. I don't even know if we're exclusive. She's super good-looking and really popular. I should be honored that she offered, right?"

"Honored?"

"I mean, she knows I'm still trying to get over Jolene. She's letting me hang around even though I have that on my mind all the time." She shrugged.

"Girl, I think you and this rebound might be using each other a little bit."

Ellie forced out a deep breath.

"Have you talked to Jolene at all since your breakup?" she asked.

"No. Not since she texted me that time."

Rose rested a hand on Ellie's shoulder. "I think you're hung up on her because you never got any real closure. Where is she? What she's doing?" Rose asked.

Ellie shook her head.

"Maybe you could convince me to Facebook-stalk her for you," Rose offered with a small shrug. "Part of the healing process is seeing an ex move on and then realizing that you have to be better than them and force yourself to move on even faster."

"That sounds wrong," Ellie groaned.

"Oh, no, believe me. I am very, very right," Rose assured.

"But I thought trying something with Sylvia would force me to move on."

"Hey, that works for some people. It's just that you're not like those people."

"So?"

"So, I think you need to call it quits with this Sylvia until you work out your own way of moving on," Rose said with another squeeze to her shoulder.

"I don't know where to start," she admitted.

Rose ambled over to the coffee dispensers again. She poured herself a new cup of something richer and perched on the edge of the stool, looking intently into Ellie's eyes.

"I think the key for you will be focusing on what you're doing after college. Have you applied for any jobs yet?"

Ellie shook her head. She had a million tabs open on her computer of all the museums she dreamed of one day working at. But she hadn't sent cover letters to any of them. She was paralyzed, stuck with too many options and avenues. She explained her reasoning to Rose.

"What's your number one dream job?" her boss asked.

"The Smithsonian," she answered without hesitation.

"Do they have any jobs?"

"A few. But I don't think I'm really qualified."

Rose waved the negativity away. "Bullshit! Bring me a cover letter for the job you want there and I'll proofread it. We'll send it off and hope for the best. And then we'll repeat the process until we're both satisfied that one of them will hire you. Okay?" she asked.

Ellie gave Rose a bone-crushing hug.

"Really?"

"Yes, really. I read, like, a thousand résumés every year for this crappy place. I know my way around an application," she boasted.

"I don't think it's crappy," Ellie joked as she pulled back.

"You haven't been here long enough. Give it a few more years," she muttered.

They both chuckled. Rose's look grew more serious.

"The Smithsonian would be lucky to have you. We'll make it happen," she promised.

Ellie knew Rose couldn't promise such a lofty future. Still, she felt blessed that her boss cared enough to help her try for her dreams. Maybe this was the first step to moving on.

CHAPTER THIRTY-TWO

Who knew MLA citations would come in handy?

Jolene scribbled through an error on the fact sheet, thankful that all her professors had stressed the use of proper citations from day one at Jones University. She opened her top drawer for a spare pad of Post-It notes and read through the document a second time, making note of errors. Once finished, she bounded out of her chair to cross the makeshift bullpen and knock on the campaign manager's door.

"Come," she heard through the rough grain.

She entered the small office. Her heartbeat picked up a bit as she cleared her throat.

"I have the revisions on today's statement and fact sheet, sir," she explained as she handed the documents over.

"Great. Go get started on those tax figures on Jim's desk," said the candidate. He reached for the papers.

"Yes sir." She left without hesitation.

As she moved through the chaos to get her next assignment, Jolene took a moment to be thankful of where she stood. It had been three weeks since she had joined the campaign. She was cautious to think of this as her destiny, but she woke up each day with an idea of what she needed to do in order to make the world a different, if not a better, place. She still wasn't nearly high enough up the political food chain for her liking, but she made a difference on a small scale day after day. It might be slight, but she knew her addition to the team was a bonus.

"Jo?" someone asked, which startled her from her musings.

"Yeah," she answered to another staffer overloaded by thick files.

"Could you help me organize these for a sec?" the girl asked.

Sarah was a petite thing, with a perfectly cut and highlighted bob and high heels that looked deadly. She was whip-smart and cunning and had quickly become Jolene's friend on the campaign trail.

"Sure," she offered.

She took half the files and followed Sarah to her desk.

"What are they?" she asked as they settled in the rickety office chairs.

"Donor files. Once they're alphabetized, I have to make a spreadsheet. I think they want to put pressure on anyone who hasn't donated yet this month," Sarah said.

"Sounds fun," Jolene goaded.

"Maybe. Definitely more fun than cold calls."

Jolene knew the truth of that statement. Her first three days had been all cold calls. After about thirty minutes she knew it wasn't the job for her. But, after the countless hang-ups and tirades, she had gotten her first break. She casually brought attention to a flaw in a speech on women's initiatives over a coffee break and her boss had given her the opportunity to rewrite the entire section. Jolene figured she got the task because she was a Jones grad but didn't care; the assignment had already opened doors for her, like not being asked to cold call.

"Any plans this weekend?" Sarah asked.

"No. I think I'll be sleeping as much as possible."

"Good choice."

"What about you?" she asked, sure that Sarah would be out doing something. She didn't think the other woman ever went home.

"Well, I'm thinking I might drive out to see my little brother in Rutland."

"That's kind of far. Birthday?"

"No. I think I'm going to miss his graduation next month because of this"—she gestured around them— "so I figured I would go sooner rather than later." Take him out to lunch and ruffle his hair, the whole thing. You only graduate high school once, right?"

Jolene slipped another file into order. "That's sweet of you," she mused.

She hadn't realized graduation was so soon. Her thoughts drifted to Ellie again, as they often did. Ellie would soon be donning her cap and gown, along with the rest of her graduating class. Jolene felt a pang. She wished she could be there to see Ellie walk across the stage and receive her diploma. She imagined the bright expression that would completely overtake Ellie's features as she shook hands with the university president. She felt pride well up inside. Unfortunately, she wouldn't be there. Jolene refocused on the task before her.

"What's up, Jo?"

"Hm?" she asked, roused from her thoughts.

"You seem preoccupied. Alphabetizing too easy for you?" Sarah joked.

"No, it's not that. You just made me remember something," Jolene responded.

"Something good?"

Jolene winced. "Not really."

"Cryptic. Well, now you have to explain."

"I really need to get back to the tax figures." Jolene thumbed toward Jim's desk piled high with work to be tackled. She didn't think she was ready for this conversation.

"Oh please. The boss never leaves his office. You can spare ten minutes to vent with me. As long as you want to, though!

I'm not trolling for office gossip, if that's what you're worried about," Sarah clarified.

Jolene took a deep breath. If she were honest with herself, she could use someone to talk to for a few minutes.

"Well, the short version is that my ex-girlfriend is graduating this month and I'm still hung up on her. I guess you talking about your trip kind of made me start daydreaming about making a trip of my own. But it's silly. It's my fault that we broke up and she wouldn't want me there." She trailed off.

Jolene thought about how Ellie's eyes had brimmed with tears during their last conversation. She wanted to erase that memory more than anything in the world.

"How do you know she doesn't want you there?" Sarah questioned as she sorted another file into place.

"I texted her before I left campus and she never responded."

"Well, that doesn't mean anything."

Jolene looked up. "It means an awful lot to me," she replied tersely.

"No, I mean—" Sarah spluttered before starting again, "— texting is a really cold way of communicating. It's easy to say 'sorry' or 'goodbye' or 'I love you' through a little screen. It's a whole different matter when you have to do it face-to-face."

Jolene let that idea sink in for a minute. Sarah had a point, but even though she missed Ellie like crazy, a tiny part of her didn't want to face these emotions or face Ellie. Letting things fester might just be easier.

"I don't want to get rejected," Jolene admitted.

"Who does?" Sarah asked flippantly. "The problem with your logic is that if you don't try and apologize in person, you can never know if things have the potential to change."

"So, you're saying I should drive to another state, surprise my ex-girlfriend—a girl whose heart I mangled by a lie of omission right before finals—and then ask for a second chance?"

"Well, yeah. I guess that about sums it up."

"It sounds like a recipe for disaster," Jolene said.

"Or great make-up sex," Sarah said cockily.

Jolene burst into laughter. Sarah doubled over as well, which caused nearby campaign workers to look up from their computer screens. Their laughs only grew louder when they realized they were causing a scene.

"Ladies! Do I have to separate you?" their boss boomed from his doorway.

Jolene's eyes snapped up. "No sir!" she answered in as professional a voice as possible.

"Get back to work," he ordered as he closed the door again with a loud thump.

Jolene stood up to go grab her next assignment off Jim's desk. Sarah wiped tears from her eyes.

"Thanks. I'll think about it," Jolene said.

"I'm chock-full of advice, so ask anytime!" Sarah replied kindly.

CHAPTER THIRTY-THREE

Don't make eye contact.

Ellie hadn't noticed Jolene's friends in the dining hall until after she rounded the salad bar. She took a deep breath and tried to slip past the table without being noticed. She heard Mo's voice as she passed by.

"Hi Ellie."

Mo and Natalie looked at her with sincerity written in every feature. Her attempt to sneak by them had been completely selfish, Ellie realized. These women hadn't done anything to hurt her and, once upon a time, she thought they were all on their way to becoming friends.

"Hi," she answered.

Natalie put down her fork and pushed the chair next to her out from under the table.

"Do you want to join us?"

There wasn't anyone else waiting for her. Maybe it was time to face this head on. She muttered her thanks as she put down her plate.

"It's no problem," Mo replied carefully. "We've been hoping to catch up with you, actually. Figured your dining hall was the best place to find you."

Ellie shrugged halfheartedly. She felt brittle. It seemed like her acquaintances measured every word before they spoke; even every move seemed calculated. She didn't want pity or sympathy from Jolene's friends. She knew it wasn't their fault that her heart had been ripped to shreds. Her guess was that they wanted her to give them a sign that it was okay to treat her normally. She cleared her throat and tried to muster the strength to do so.

"How are you guys doing?" Ellie asked. "Enjoying your last semester so far?"

Mo and Natalie shared a look. It seemed like some unspoken signal was being passed between them. Mo was the first to turn back to Ellie.

"Good. I've been spending a lot of time staring at textbooks, like most of the other seniors at the moment. Natalie keeps asking me to proofread her thesis. It's getting to be a pain."

Natalie rolled her eyes. "She secretly loves it."

Ellie felt a tug at the corner of her mouth. She really liked Jolene's friends—yet another thing her ex-girlfriend had effortlessly taken from her.

"I don't know what makes you think that," Mo complained. "I am clearly a very busy lady. I would much rather be reading my assignments instead of thousands of words about Chaucer. I hated Chaucer all the way back in high school."

"And I am trying to change that about you with exposure therapy," Natalie emphasized. Natalie's piercing gaze made Ellie feel instantly unsettled. "How are you, Ellie?"

Ellie breathed out harshly and noted too late that she sounded slightly shaken. She ducked her head down and glared at the sad salad still on her plate. What did she have to lose by being honest?

"I'm doing okay, I guess. As well as can be expected. It's been hard." She watched the other girls nod. "I still miss her. All the time."

"We're really sorry about what happened," Mo said quietly. It was the softest Ellie had ever heard her speak. Of course, Jolene would have sensitive friends. She felt tears threaten to well up, but blinked a few times to clear her vision.

"I'm sorry, Ellie," Natalie added. "I warned her that something like this could happen, but I think she was too wrapped up in the moment to realize how much damage she was doing." She paused and sighed deeply. "I'm not trying to make excuses for her. I think she fucked up something great. And I'm sure she thinks so too. I just—"

"We," Mo interrupted.

"Yeah," Natalie continued, "we just want you to know that if you need someone to talk to or even someone to *not* talk to about it—we're here."

Emotion rushed over Ellie. She smiled at the women opposite her. Kind people would always offer support when you needed it. She bit her lip as she tried to stop its wobble at the thought that even though she had only eaten one meal with Natalie and Mo before the breakup, they both were still willing to offer help. It meant so much and her only reaction was a fresh wave of almost-tears. To try to preserve some sense of pride, she quickly dabbed her napkin at the corner of her eyes.

"Thank you. Both of you," she mumbled. Mo squeezed her hand. The warmth and kindness of the touch made Ellie think of Sylvia, and how her fling never touched her with such reverence or care.

In that moment, she knew things with Sylvia had to end. Rose had been right. The weird parasitic relationship they had formed over the past month wasn't good for either of them in the long run. Ellie had other things to worry about, like working on her job applications and their final a cappella performance of the year. She could make it to the end of the semester in one piece with the help of people like Rose, Natalie and Mo. Sylvia could—and probably would—only bring her down. Clarity lifted the weight. It was the right decision. It was something she needed to do for herself, and she needed to do it soon.

CHAPTER THIRTY-FOUR

This is not good.

Jolene refreshed her tab again in hopes of a different result. The *Burlington Free Press* had just called the election in the opponent's favor. She looked up at the television across the bullpen to see the local affiliate doing the same.

"Shit," she heard echo from behind her.

Sarah flopped down into her squeaky desk chair.

"Well, I guess we're out of a job," she offered with a shrug.

"Yeah. Too bad, I just figured out how to work that dumb copier," Sarah joked.

Jolene reclined in her own chair and let her eyes track the peeling paint on the ceiling. She needed to go home and sleep for a week to make up for all the hours she had lost during the campaign. Still, she knew if she went home now she would just end up staring at a different ceiling. Her mind still raced with thoughts of the election and what would come next.

"Well, I know one good thing that came of this," Sarah admitted.

Jolene looked over with a raised eyebrow.

"You have the time off to go see that girl you're still pining over." Jolene pinched her temples, sure that a headache would soon appear.

"I don't know."

"Oh, come on! What else could you possibly have to do this week that is more important? *House of Cards* marathon?"

"Please, I'm one hundred percent up-to-date on that show."

"Well, don't try and distract me with a discussion about theories for next season. You have to go apologize to that poor girl!"

Jolene thought about the possibilities. A memory of Ellie's smile sparked something inside her. She felt her heart swell at the idea that maybe things could be different.

"I guess there's only one way to find out, right?" she asked.

"Yep," Sarah agreed. "Now get a move on. There's nothing left for you here in this elephant graveyard of an office."

Jolene felt suddenly lighter. She was halfway through a mental checklist of what she would need for the trip. She thanked Sarah as she grabbed her shoulder bag and jacket.

"Go on! Get out of here! I'll email you if anything comes up," Sarah said cheerily.

Jolene practically ran to the elevator, avoiding coworkers consoling each other over the upset; clumps of people were still gathered in front of the television as if the results might somehow change. Not likely. She was disappointed at the loss, but really, there was so much more that awaited her outside the office.

As she stepped into the elevator, Jolene sent a text to Natalie and Mo, sure they would still be awake—either focused on their final assignments or distracted with a Disney movie marathon.

Hey guys. Any room for a newly unemployed friend to crash on your floor tomorrow night?

By the time Jolene was in the parking lot, she had received a reply from Mo.

YES?!?? Come do all my work for me!!! Please?! :)

Clearly, her friend was in panic mode. It was understandable, with only three days of classes left before the short respite of reading period. Finals would be back at Jones University before they knew it.

No. But I can do moral support!

Jolene hopped in the car and started the drive to her small apartment, excited at the prospect of tomorrow. Her mind returned to the image of Ellie right before Jolene had left her dorm room for the last time. Why hadn't she stayed and fought for herself? For their relationship? This time, things would be different. For the first time in months, Jolene felt a glimmer of hope. Maybe she could change her future after all.

CHAPTER THIRTY-FIVE

Okay, now's the moment.

Sylvia glanced up from her phone when Ellie cleared her throat.

"Hey. That dress looks good on you." Sylvia looked back down at the bright screen.

Ellie had attempted to end her fling with Sylvia for the past three days, all to no avail. Each time, she had gone to Rose and shared the story of her failure. And each time, Rose had listened perceptively and then assured her that she was doing the right thing. It didn't help anyone to continue to put effort into a relationship without a solid foundation. Ellie knew what Rose was trying to say, but she still had trouble with the breakup conversation. But now she had run out of time. Ellie found it ironic that she was now having trouble verbalizing her concerns to Sylvia in the same way that Jolene had failed to tell her the truth all those months ago. She now understood why Jolene had put it off. It was easier to stay quiet than to just come out with the truth.

"Can I talk to you for a minute?" Ellie began.

"Now?"

"Yeah, if that's okay."

"Sure, but the rest of the group should be here in a few minutes," Sylvia explained as she flipped her long turquoise hair onto her shoulder.

"Can you put your phone down for a second?" Ellie asked with measured politeness. Sylvia looked up again, this time with suspicion. Apparently, Ellie's attempt at politeness was lost on her.

"What's got your panties in a twist?" came the sharp reply.

Ellie figured it was now or never.

"I think we should stop hooking up—or whatever it is we're doing. I think we're two very different people and I don't see this going in a direction that I want to go. It's a really awkward time—"

"Yeah! I'll say!" Sylvia retorted. She stood up from her lazy perch on the small sofa.

"Well, I just mean that I don't think it was fair for either one of us to be stringing the other along. Especially since reading period starts tomorrow and finals are on Monday. I think it's for the best if we just stop now."

"Really?" Sylvia asked, her voice taking on an edge that Ellie hadn't heard from her before.

"Really what?" Ellie was unsure of what Sylvia meant.

"You're breaking things off because you have too much homework." Distaste dripped from every word.

"No, that's not—" Ellie ventured, but then caught herself up short. A few of their group members trickled into the room.

"Jesus Ellie," Sylvia snarled. "I've been walking on eggshells around you for weeks trying to let you work out your problems; I'd hoped you'd just get over it and actually fuck me like an adult. After all that work you're gonna break things off with me?"

"What?" Ellie spluttered.

The other girls stopped in their tracks, realizing that they had just walked into the middle of a surprisingly heated argument. Ellie didn't understand Sylvia's point but she had witnessed too many of Sylvia's blowups with Alyssa to misread the girl who stood across the room from her now. Sylvia was completely serious and they were only a razor's edge from dangerous territory. Ellie thought breaking up would be the adult thing to do. She should have realized that Sylvia would jump at the opportunity to turn it into an event for the whole group to witness.

"You put way too much effort into your work when you should have been working on how to keep a girl happy. Maybe that's why your last girlfriend left you." Sylvia's accusation stung.

Ellie tried to calm herself with a deep breath. Sylvia only lashed out to hurt others and make a scene so she could be the center of attention. She remembered Rose's reassurances. She wouldn't let Sylvia's accusations derail her resolve.

"I'm not putting my grades before you, Sylvia. I'm putting myself first for once."

"Yeah, right! All you ever talk about is your feelings. How you miss that girl that broke your heart and how you want so badly to graduate with honors and work at that fucking museum. You need to grow up," Sylvia sneered, edging closer to Ellie with each word.

"Is it so bad to have a dream? A goal in life?" she asked.

"Not if it means putting yourself above other people who count on you! Look what you're doing to the group." She waved at the girls frozen in the doorway. "Why couldn't you have waited until after the performance to drag all this up?"

"I don't know," Ellie answered. She looked back at the group but, to her shock, instead of disdain or derision, her friends cheered her on.

"Yeah, exactly," Sylvia said with a snarl.

Ellie looked into Sylvia's eyes. "Actually, I do know why. Because every moment I spend with you is another moment that you are just holding me back from becoming my best self. I shouldn't have to justify my dreams to you. You should understand that it's what I want and then you should support me. That's what a real girlfriend would do. It's what a real Jones student would do."

"I hate to break it to you, but you're not my girlfriend. We were just fooling around," Sylvia responded.

"Maybe you're right. But if I mean nothing to you, then this conversation shouldn't bother you at all," she reasoned. "So, if that's the case, let's start warming up for the jam."

"You're unbelievable. I'm over this. Good luck performing without your best soloist, bitches," Sylvia replied. She turned and stormed through the group of girls still huddled in the doorway, transfixed as if by a train wreck. They looked to Ellie and waited for some sign that the smoke had cleared.

"I'm sorry, guys. I didn't think she would explode like that," she admitted as she flopped down onto the couch.

A few girls shrugged as they made their way into the room.

"She was always an asshole," Gabrielle murmured sagely.

That remark caused a few titters from the group.

"I think we're better off without her," their newest member added as she dropped her bag to the floor.

"Do you think she'll come back?" one of the first-years asked.

"No. I don't think so," Ellie answered.

That's when it really sunk in. Their president and lead vocalist had just stormed out fifteen minutes before their final jam of the year. They had spent the past two months in preparation for this event and Ellie had destroyed it in seconds.

"Shit," Gabrielle blurted, the same realization written clearly on her face.

"Yeah, that about sums it up," Ellie agreed.

She collected her thoughts as the silence stretched on. It only took her a moment to decide that she wouldn't let Sylvia ruin this event for her or the other members of the Jones Tones.

"All right, let's form a plan to make this the best jam of the year—with or without our asshole president."

Devilish looks all around the room led Ellie to believe they might actually pull it off. Probably.

CHAPTER THIRTY-SIX

Breathe.

Jolene gulped in the warm evening air as she walked under the archway that led to the largest auditorium on campus. Natalie and Mo were on either side of her, and offered silent support as they made their way to the final a cappella jam of the year. The Jones Tones were one of the most popular groups on campus, evidenced by the throngs of people that poured into the building. Despite the looming presence of finals, students from all over campus had taken time out of their schedules for one last opportunity to celebrate and let go. Jolene felt herself relax. In just a few minutes she would see Ellie again.

"What's got you so cheerful?" Mo asked knowingly.

"Isn't it obvious?" Natalie said.

Jolene glanced at her friends and sent up a silent thank you to the universe for their continued presence in her life. She had spent the last two nights camped out on Mo's dusty floor. Her days had been consumed with long stretches of time alone in the dorm room; she'd eaten bad dining hall food that her friends had pilfered for her. The only bright spot had been an email from Sarah. Apparently, back at campaign headquarters, an offer to return to work was in the wind, but Jolene instantly placed it on the back burner. Instead, she finished a novel and rewatched the only season of *Commander in Chief* while cooped up in the small room. But most of the time, she wondered about Ellie. Where was she and what was she doing? Would she be working at the café? Or maybe she would have traded shifts with other students to free up her time for last-minute studying. What song would she perform at the jam? Would she be beatboxing again?

Jolene's heart fluttered as she realized all her answers would be answered soon enough. She had planned every sentence she would say to Ellie. All she had to do was wait for the concert to end and the applause to finish. After that, she would walk right up to her and apologize, explain herself and, if things went well, ask for a second chance.

"It's going to be fine," Natalie assured her as she rested her strong hand on Jolene's shoulder.

Jolene hoped her friend was right. The women walked into the venue and found three seats together near the back, which suited Jolene perfectly since she planned to stay out of Ellie's line of sight until after the performance. Jolene sandwiched herself between Natalie and Mo, instantly comforted by their warm shoulders pressed against hers. Nothing could be better than woman support.

The lights dimmed as the last stragglers took their seats around the room. Before Jolene could run through her mental plan again, the Jones Tones walked onto the small stage. Her heart stuttered as her eyes found Ellie, in the same black dress she had worn to the jam that had brought them together. The last time she had seen that dress, it had been crumpled on the floor next to her own clothes. The blue neckerchief was tied on Ellie's wrist, adding the pop of color that all Jones Tones members were known to wear during performances. As Ellie moved across the stage, Jolene started to reminisce about their late-night walks after Ellie's shifts at the café. She remembered how their hands had fit together. Her eyes caught at the nape of Ellie's neck, where her hair brushed against her skin and freckles. In her head, she listened to the echo of Ellie's laugh, a bubble of memory of watching a terrible movie together curled up in her dorm room. She felt herself aching to get up and reach out for the woman she loved. How had she ever left this woman behind?

"Where's Sylvia?" Natalie's whisper jolted Jolene from her thoughts.

"What?" she asked dazedly.

"Sylvia! Their president! The hot one with the undercut?" Natalie continued.

Jolene looked at the rest of the group and noticed that they were one short. Sylvia was a major player in the a cappella community at Jones.

"Did she graduate with me?" Jolene asked.

"No, I have a class with her this semester," Mo added.

"That's not good. She usually has, like, at least three solos," Jolene said. Her eyes wandered around the room.

At the microphone, Ellie waved at the large audience.

"Hi everyone! We're the Jones Tones. Welcome to our final jam of the year!"

Her introduction was met with screams and whistles as the audience settled in for their last bit of fun before finals.

"We have a great set prepared for you all tonight, but we ask for your patience as you bear with us." She paused until the audience hushed. "We are down one senior Toner tonight, someone many of you probably came to see," she explained.

A ripple moved through the crowd and Jolene heard a few murmurs of disappointment.

"Still, if Jones teaches us anything, it's to persevere in the face of unexpected obstacles like missing group members or impossibly difficult exams," she continued brightly.

That brought a holler from the audience.

"So, without further ado, here are the Jones Tones!" she said as she swept an arm out toward the other singers dressed in black behind her. She joined the loose semicircle to loud cheers from the audience.

"You picked one hell of a girl to love," Mo whispered.

"I know," Jolene admitted. "I just hope she still loves me back."

The group waited for the audience to quiet before Ellie's right hand started to mark the beat of their first number.

As the first notes resonated out over the crowd, Jolene was transported. Ellie's foot tapped the rhythm, as constant as her own heartbeat, and calmed once she recognized Ellie's own high voice from amongst all the others. Her eyes slipped closed as she listened to the music wash over her. Each song ended with wild cheers from the crowd. The group had adapted to the loss of their president almost flawlessly. A shy first-year stepped forward to take over one of the *Crazy in Love* solos usually reserved for their absent member. Her surprised friends in the second row went wild as she belted out the opening lyrics. Camera phones were held up for nearly every song, and even one student who waved a lighter during their homage to Celine Dion. Ellie stayed at the edge of the semicircle, always playing the role of pitch. She let others take her old solos so she could continue being the heartbeat for the group. Her beatboxing skills were on display for a new Avril Lavigne number and Jolene looked on admiringly, convinced that Ellie had improved even more since the last jam. The set flew by and Ellie was back in front of the microphone.

"Thank you all for coming." She motioned for the audience to quiet down. This useless effort only stirred more whoops from the rowdier women in the room, with one particularly loud eruption from the front.

"I love you, girl!"

"Thanks boss!" Ellie winked at the audience. Jolene chuckled, sure that Rose wouldn't have missed this performance for all the coffee in the world.

"Our last song of the set was supposed to be a mash-up of Passenger's *Let Her Go* and Bastille's *Pompeii*, but—" she looked at her group standing behind her as the crowd cheered—"I don't think we can do it without Sylvia."

The audience let out a disappointed groan.

"Isn't that the mash-up you helped her with?" Mo asked as she grabbed Jolene's knee roughly.

"Yeah," Jolene answered suspiciously.

"Go up there!" she demanded.

"What?" Jolene asked.

She looked back up at the stage. Ellie glanced uncertainly at the other soloists in her group. They talked in hushed whispers as the crowd continued to urge them to perform the song.

"Go! Now's your chance!" Mo explained.

"But—" she objected.

"Mo's right, it would be quite an entrance, to say the least," Natalie added.

Jolene saw the sudden appeal of her friends' harebrained scheme, but she had already rehearsed exactly what she was going to say to Ellie after the concert. This wasn't part of the plan. Ellie stepped back in front of the microphone.

"Yeah, sorry guys, but we're going to close the show with our old Taylor Swift medley instead. It's just not possible without the whole group," she frowned.

"Wait!" Jolene felt herself yell as she stood up from her seat.

She saw Ellie squint out over the crowd to see who had yelled.

"Sylvia?" she asked into the microphone.

Jolene practically leapt over the two girls seated at the end of her row. She sprinted up the center aisle. There was no way to turn back now. She took one last deep breath as she stepped up onto the small stage.

"No, not Sylvia," she offered, not sure of what else to say.

Ellie's eyes widened. The restless crowd began to murmur.

"What are you doing here?" Ellie asked, shock written across her face.

"I came to see you."

"Why?" she asked.

"What do you say we talk about it after we sing your mash-up?" she answered.

Ellie looked at the crowd, dazed as they began to shout and clap wildly at the unexpected turn of events. She snapped out of it and glanced once more at Jolene.

"All right everyone, this is Jolene. She's an Acapellago alum and she's going to help us out on this one." Cheers erupted once again as Jolene moved closer to Ellie. Once close enough to share the microphone, she looked up and waited for her cue.

Ellie counted in the group, and the first few notes of *Pompeii* started to rise from half of the women behind them. Jolene thought back to the night that Ellie had explained her idea for this mash-up. They had huddled over the lyrics together and discussed how best to arrange it for the Jones Tones. Jolene remembered it like it was yesterday, even though she had never actually heard it. She had understood its potential that night, but now—hearing it surround her while an audience waited on edge—she realized its true brilliance.

Ellie's beautiful voice washed over her as she softly started her solo. With each word, the voice gained strength.

Jolene pictured it, the months they had been apart and the hurt she had caused without a thought. Ellie seemed to pour her heart out into those words as she kept the song moving. Jolene leaned in toward the microphone, catching Ellie's eye as she joined the song with her own part. She let all her apologies and fears seep into her words. She looked deep into Ellie's glassy eyes and knew she understood. Their voices blended in the space between them. The audience was rapt with hushed attention. Their voices harmonized perfectly as they joined together to sing the final chorus about love and letting go, about optimism despite being hurt, and about walls that tumbled to allow someone else in.

As the final beats faded, Ellie looked at Jolene with raw emotion written deep in her features. She saw the pain, but more than that, she saw hope just under the surface. She smiled at Ellie as she heard the audience go wild.

Jolene turned to face the crowd and took a small bow with the rest of the Jones Tones. Natalie and Mo were on their feet, as they clapped loudly and screamed her name. She waved a thank you and walked toward her seat, but felt a warm hand grasp her own.

Ellie was focused intently on their intertwined fingers. Their eyes met again and Jolene felt a small glimmer of hope.

She had waited so long to be this close to Ellie again. Too long, she realized.

"I'm sorry," she stuttered, aware that she had launched straight to the end of her planned apology over the din of the crowd.

"Okay," Ellie offered as she pulled Jolene in. Their lips met roughly at first, but the wolf whistles from the crowd and sharp edges of the kiss faded away as the kiss deepened. She had missed these lips and this woman. This was the most right thing in the world and she would do anything to keep Ellie in her life. Ellie pulled back, squeezed Jolene's fingers tightly, and pulled her off stage and through the door.

CHAPTER THIRTY-SEVEN

Don't let her go!

Ellie felt her control slip away. Her fingers had lost circulation from the way they dug into Jolene's wrist as she pulled her further and further backstage. The last five minutes had been a whirlwind of emotion. Her heart thumped loudly in her ears from the combination of Jolene's sudden reappearance, the final solo of her college career and the kiss.

That kiss. It was what Ellie had dreamed of for months, but more than that, she wanted to corner Jolene, ask her to explain what had happened between them, and then have her beg for forgiveness. She let herself mull over those odds as she guided Jolene into a supply closet at the end of the hallway.

She turned the lights on and shut them inside and away from the witnesses to their romantic display up on stage.

"What are you doing here?" Ellie asked again.

Jolene's eyes were earnest, even as tears started.

"I'm here to apologize," Jolene whispered.

"Go on," she said as she crossed her arms.

"I'm so sorry, El. I honestly didn't think that my early graduation would hurt you so much," she said as she stepped closer.

Ellie felt like all her words poured out as she interrupted Jolene's attempt at an apology. "That wasn't the part that upset me. I was mad because you never told me. We spent practically the whole semester as friends and half of that time we were dating, but you never mentioned that you were moving away."

"I know," Jolene replied, eyes focused on her black boots.

"You moved across the country!"

"Yes."

"Why?" Ellie asked.

"I went to work for my grandparents," she began.

"No, I meant—" Ellie sighed. "Why didn't you tell me?"

"I guess I was scared that you would break things off once you found out. I guess avoiding the problem seemed easier than talking about it," Jolene admitted.

"Well, look where that got us."

"I know."

Ellie hated seeing Jolene like this. She wouldn't make eye contact. Instead she stared down intently as she scraped a boot into the linoleum. She looked so small compared to Ellie's memory of her. The proud and confident woman she had loved wasn't here. The replacement that stood hunched in front of her was nervous and unsure.

"Look at me, Jo."

Jolene raised her head. Tears ran down her cheeks. "I'm so sorry," Jolene cried.

"I'm sure you are," Ellie acknowledged.

"Can you ever forgive me?" she asked through a new wave of tears.

Ellie rested a hand on Jolene's cheek. Despite having her heart broken, Ellie knew somewhere deep inside that there was more to them than this misstep. They were meant for more than a horrible misunderstanding thanks to poor communication.

"Yes."

Jolene blinked up at her and choked back a stifled sob. Ellie felt her heart break all over again.

"Oh god." Jolene wept as she clutched to Ellie.

Ellie's hand cupped the back of Jolene's head and felt the soft hair under her fingers as tears soaked into her collar. Jolene continued to murmur *I'm sorry* quietly again and again as she held the woman in her arms. When the tears subsided, Ellie pulled back from the hug to look at Jolene.

"I'm so glad you're here," she admitted.

"Me too," Jolene answered, despite her wet cheeks and snotty nose.

Ellie untied the blue scarf from her wrist and handed it to Jolene. She quickly wiped her face and blew her nose.

"Sorry," she said with a grimace as she tried to hand the soggy fabric back.

"It's okay. I don't need it anymore. Last performance, remember?"

Jolene clumsily folded the scarf and stuffed it into her pocket.

Ellie hesitated, still nervous and unsure, but no longer in search of an escape route. She moved closer, pulled Jolene's chin up, and leaned in to kiss Jolene again—this time without the crowd to watch. She felt the soft lips open under her own and wondered how she could have ever let Jolene go.

"Will you walk me home?" Ellie asked.

"Of course."

They walked across campus, hand in hand. The summer air brushed against them, still cool enough to feel like a caress. Many students stopped to congratulate them on their performance and moaned how the Jones Tones would never be able to top that final duet. Ellie received the compliments appreciatively, but wondered about the many unanswered questions that still simmered between her and Jolene.

What had Jolene been doing since she'd left Jones?

Ellie also knew she would have to explain why Sylvia had ditched the concert. She wouldn't be happy to have that conversation, but knew it would be important to be honest about everything if they wanted to start fresh. She couldn't let them go down that road twice.

"Are you freaking out about exams?" Jolene asked, finally breaking the tension between them.

"Not really. Two of my finals are papers that I have mostly finished already. I think the professors go a little easier on everyone during the spring semester," she explained.

"Oh, now you tell me!" Jolene joked.

Ellie smiled, aware of the spirit of their relationship that waited at the edge of each word they spoke. If she let it happen, they could go back to the way they had been before. The real question was whether going back was the good thing to do. Her thoughts rested on the possibilities. In two weeks Ellie would be a Jones graduate too. Other than that, she was still unsure of what would be waiting for her afterward. Maybe all she needed was a friendly face ready to greet her on the other side.

Jolene came to a stop when they reached Ellie's dorm, uncertainty back in her eyes.

"Do you want to come in and talk?" Ellie asked.

"Yeah, if that's okay with you."

"I think it would help."

She fished her keycard out of her bag and let Jolene inside. They walked the two flights up to her room and she led the way to her door. She found a letter taped to her whiteboard with a small note scribbled in the corner.

Hey Ellie. Special delivery from the mailman! (It looks important!)

She looked more closely at the letter addressed to her and recognized the small insignia in the top corner.

"Oh my god!"

"What?" Jolene asked, peeking over her shoulder.

"It's from the Smithsonian," she answered, completely dazed.

"You applied!" Jolene gasped.

Time stopped for Ellie as she looked down at the letter in her hands, terrified of its contents.

"You have to open it," Jolene encouraged.

"I know," she murmured, but her hands wouldn't move.

"Do you need a letter opener?"

"What?" Ellie finally looked up from the white rectangle that could change her life.

"I'm sure it's good news! You shouldn't be afraid to open it," Jolene offered calmly.

Ellie shook her head. She looked down again and ripped the envelope open before she could hesitate another second. She unfolded the creamy paper and read the first line and then immediately dropped the paper. Her eyes met Jolene's and she felt herself fill with joy.

"I got it! I got the job!" she screamed.

Jolene gathered Ellie up in strong arms and hugged her until it felt like all the air was pressed out of her lungs. "Congratulations, El! That's amazing!" she said.

"Oh my god. I can't believe it. I guess that means I'm moving to DC." Tremors ran through her limbs at the prospect. Her first thought was that she needed to tell Rose. Her dreams had come true and it wouldn't have been possible without her boss's support, almost daily lectures about self-worth, and constant motivation. She couldn't believe that she was going to work at the Smithsonian. It was unbelievable, and yet she had confidence that it was the perfect step for her to take.

"That's funny." Jolene interrupted her thoughts.

Ellie bent down to pick the letter back up off the dingy carpet, and then opened the door to her room. "What's funny?"

"I'm moving there too."

Her eyes snapped back to Jolene, who sheepishly held one arm braced against her middle as if she had to hold herself together.

"You are?"

"Yeah. My friend and I got job offers yesterday for a campaign in DC. I haven't told them I'll do it yet, but I think it might be the place for me."

Ellie sat down on her bed before her legs gave out from under her. How had so much changed so quickly? In one day her whole future had changed. All the doors that she assumed had been closed months ago were suddenly wide open.

"You're not moving there because of me, right?" she asked worriedly.

"Well," Jolene hesitated, "I would be lying if I said it didn't matter."

"Okay," Ellie breathed, trying to gather her wits.

"I'm sorry if I really sprung this whole thing on you. I didn't mean to do it this way. I just showed up to apologize and maybe talk a little bit. You should be celebrating your job!"

"No, no. It's all important." Ellie paused. "You're important."

Jolene looked back at her earnestly. Ellie patted a spot on the bed next to her, and Jolene joined her. "Let's talk about the future," she said.

CHAPTER THIRTY-EIGHT

This is some heavy stuff!

"Only two more to go!" Ellie cheered.

Jolene looked around as she reentered the dorm room and realized that Ellie was right. They were nearly done. She straightened to her full height and rolled her shoulders, which caused a loud pop.

As soon as Ellie's last final had been completed, all her focus had shifted to packing up her dorm room and all the memories it contained. Jolene had spent finals week in DC to find an apartment and sign the contract for her new job. Then she drove back to East Westwick.

They were still on tenuous ground; Jolene was encouraged when Ellie immediately agreed to put her to work. They spent the morning together and packed most of Ellie's belongings. Only two empty boxes remained. Jolene graciously volunteered to be the one to carry everything down the two flights to the car. She regretted the choice once she realized just how many textbooks Ellie had planned to take with her to DC.

"Thank god this is all you have," Jolene mused.

"Oh, it's not that bad."

"You say that now, but I think you'll change your tune once I make you take them all out of the car," she answered slyly.

"I have muscles!" Ellie boasted as she flexed a bicep.

"Oh yeah?" Jolene crossed the room to pinch the flesh between her fingers. Ellie yelped in surprise and then tilted back against the bed frame behind her.

"I'm going to miss this place," she said in a hushed tone. "It really has felt like home to me."

Jolene understood what Ellie meant. Jones University had been an accepting place for Ellie, the constant in her life when her family had turned away and when Jolene had left her behind. The thought still smarted, but she tried not to dwell on the pain hidden there. She and Jolene were about to start a new chapter; if they were lucky, there wouldn't be enough time to pick at the scar that they both shared.

"I'll miss it too," she admitted. "Maybe not the dining hall food though."

"You're going to miss it once you have to cook for yourself." Ellie's smile spread wide across her face.

The spark between them had just begun to rekindle. They had stayed up all night to talk after Jolene had crashed the jam. They touched on everything they had childishly skipped over the first time, which included Ellie's concerns about being lied to and her anxiety about being left behind, as well as Jolene's desire to learn more about Ellie's family. Jolene was sure that their relationship was being rebuilt on stronger ground than before. She would be forever grateful to Ellie for a second chance. She refocused on Ellie's words and tried not to get lost in the blue eyes that followed her every move.

"I make a mean bowl of cereal," she joked. Ellie's eyes crinkled in response. "What do you have left?" She looked around the room and saw only empty shelves and a bare closet.

"There's some stuff under here," Ellie answered. She patted the bed behind her. "And I think I missed that bottom desk drawer."

Jolene walked to the desk to check. The drawer was filled with spare sticky notes, a few notebooks and another few pounds of books.

"I think you read too much," she whined as she took them out.

"No such thing." Ellie shook her head.

They started to load the remaining items into the boxes at Ellie's feet. Jolene was sad to see the room lack everything that had made it Ellie's. All those personal touches that had grabbed her attention on their first night together were now strikingly absent. The movie posters were carefully rolled away. The twinkle lights had been removed and willed to someone else in the house to use in their room the following year. All the photos were packed, unceremoniously stuffed in the pages of books so they wouldn't get creased in transport. All of Ellie's most precious possessions fit in the trunk and backseat of Jolene's small car, currently parked in front of the dorm, pointed away from this dorm and toward their future.

"Tape please?" Ellie asked for the roll by Jolene's side. Jolene waited as Ellie sealed the last two boxes. Ellie stood up, hands on hips, and looked around the room. "Done."

Jolene stood, ready to carry the boxes downstairs.

"Hold on," Ellie interrupted with a hand reached out to stop Jolene. "I think I need a second before we go." Ellie sat on the bare mattress. The springs creaked underneath her. Jolene placed a reassuring arm around her waist. She remembered having a similar reaction when she had left her own dorm room for the last time, an out-of-body experience for her. She remembered how she had stopped next to her desk for one last look, equally glad to be going and upset at the prospect of having to leave a part of herself behind. Jolene briefly wondered how many Jones women had lived in this room before Ellie. Hundreds, maybe. How many of them had felt like this? Jolene's chest constricted at the thought and she felt silly for her emotional reaction to saying goodbye to someone else's dorm room. She blinked back tears.

"Uh-oh."

"What?" Ellie asked, clearly too caught up in her own thoughts to notice Jolene.

"I think you forgot something," she said.

She pointed up. Ellie's eyes followed along. The colorful stars were still stuck in haphazard constellations above their heads. She felt Ellie's chuckle through the arm that still gripped them together.

"Nope. They're staying behind."

"Why?"

"They were here when I moved in," she explained. "And I want the next person that lives here to look up one night after staying up too late to finish a paper or after spending all day thinking that they can't make it through the semester, and I want them to see the stars. I want them to look up and realize someone did it before them. It helped me on more than one occasion." Ellie's eyes traced the trails overhead.

Jolene had never put much stock in stargazing before. But, in that moment, she understood why people did. She watched Ellie's eyes sweep across the familiar shapes one last time. It was an image she would never forget. She was witnessing someone wish on a star.

Jolene closed her eyes and did the same.

CHAPTER THIRTY-NINE

Don't worry.

"You might have to ride on top," Jolene joked. As she pressed all her weight down to close the trunk of the car, Ellie let a calm breath fill her lungs. This was it. Everything was packed. Her room key was left abandoned in the lock, two flights up from where they stood. Her fellow graduates were all leaving campus, some packed with tears in their eyes, while others ran away as fast as possible with joyful banshee screams, their responsibilities forgotten in the breeze. Ellie wasn't sure where she fell on that spectrum. She had tried to be methodical and precise to make sure nothing had been left behind. But there had been a few times when she felt like she needed to cry or shout. Her heart hammered, aware that her future was still undecided. The only certainty was that she had to leave. Preferably, before she broke down in tears in front of Jolene.

"Do you need my help?" she offered, realizing that Jolene probably didn't weigh enough to force the trunk closed. After three attempts, the trunk stayed closed.

"All right. I'm ready when you are," Jolene said. Her long hair whipped wildly in the wind. Ellie let her gaze rest on the woman beside her. At least she didn't have to do it alone. Ellie's disbelief at Jolene's reappearance on campus had slowly changed into relief for a second chance. She had listened to the apologies Jolene had mumbled through tears after the jam. There hadn't been a single second when she doubted Jolene's sincerity. And, after having a week to think about it herself, she finished finals sure that she wasn't going to let Jolene go.

Graduation had been a sunny day. Jolene had helped her get into her powder blue gown and mortarboard and had repeated how proud she was too many times to recall. She had seen so many happy faces as she walked through the crowd to her seat. Friends that would never be gathered in one place again. Underclasswomen from the Jones Tones had yelled her name as she passed by in the procession. Rose's loud voice had boomed over the others as she walked across the stage. She remembered her eager claps for Natalie and Mo as they shook the university president's hand and received their own degrees. Her mother and father had been there, but it had barely registered until they had gathered her in a warm hug after the ceremony. She had cried, convinced she had made them truly proud for the first time in years. They still loved her. The moment raised a glimmer of hope that they might one day accept her unconditionally. But, the image that resonated most clearly was the sight of Jolene after the ceremony. In that moment, Ellie was certain that she had made the right choice.

"I think I'm ready," she replied, her thoughts finally quiet. She looked around at the Quad for one last time and tried to memorize every detail. She moved around the car and slipped into the passenger seat, and exhaled harshly. The end of another chapter.

Jolene settled in the driver's seat. Ellie focused on the view outside the front windshield. She felt the tears come suddenly and heard a cry spill from her mouth.

"Oh Ellie!" Jolene said as she quickly pulled her into an embrace. "It's okay. Crying is okay." Jolene soothed her quietly.

Ellie was distantly aware that she must look foolish, but Jolene's kind words and reassurance allowed her to let it go. It was okay to cry, especially on a day like today. She felt Jolene's fingers thread through her hair, the touch instantly comforting and familiar. Ellie hugged her closer, so glad that she had someone to hold her in this moment.

She pulled back. Jolene now sported a sizeable patch of tears and snot on her shoulder.

"I'm sorry," Ellie mumbled as she tried to wipe her face.

"Here." Jolene pulled a handkerchief from her pocket and held it out. "There's nothing to be sorry about," she consoled.

Ellie wiped her face and blew her nose and felt better, confident that Jolene would be the last person to judge her for her little breakdown. They had seen one another at their lowest lows. Hopefully, such displays wouldn't be common. The emotional whiplash she had experienced this year would be plenty for years to come. Ellie wiped her eyes again and looked at the handkerchief in her hands.

"This is my Jones Tones scarf!"

"Yeah. Don't worry, I washed it since the last time I cried all over it," Jolene added with a grin.

Ellie returned the smile and clutched the sodden fabric tighter.

"I'm glad you saved it," she said.

"Of course," Jolene answered, twisting the car keys between her fingers. "It means a lot to you. I figured you would need it today. Or I would need it." She beamed. "It was a pretty safe bet that one of us was going to cry."

"Yeah. I guess you're right." She leaned over to kiss her on the cheek. "Thank you, Jolene."

Her girlfriend tried to hide the just-visible blush where Ellie's lips had touched her. Ellie looked back out over the dashboard. There was only one thing to do now.

"All right. Let's go."

EPILOGUE

25 Years and Two Weeks Later.

"Can you believe it?" Ellie asked as she came up behind Jolene to rest her chin on her wife's strong shoulder.

"Not at all," Jolene replied.

Ellie was dressed in a full-length gown that clung to her curvy figure in the most distracting ways. The aqua color brought out the blue of her partner's eyes and reminded Jolene of the times she had watched Ellie perform with the Jones Tones. Those moments still stuck in her memory, despite how long ago it had been.

"I will never admit that Taylor Swift's music is now considered 'old' by students here," Ellie practically whined. Jolene couldn't help but laugh at the overly dramatic pout on Ellie's face. She dipped her head down and kissed it away.

They had spent the last half hour being serenaded by the newest Jones University a cappella group with popular hits from their years in college, but they were now free to mingle with the other guests scattered around the auditorium and on the stage.

"She'll always be first in your heart, won't she?" Jolene whimpered with a devastated look.

"No, you know who holds that place," Ellie answered with a grin. She ran her free hand along Jolene's hip and gave a light squeeze.

"Ahem."

Ellie looked up from their compromising moment to see Rose, in a 1950s inspired cocktail dress, beside them with a hand on her waist. Ellie released Jolene, pushed her drink into her wife's hand, and promptly launched herself at her former boss.

"Rose! I didn't know you would be here!" she exclaimed as Jolene looked on fondly, eyes tracing over the way Ellie's short hair swayed as it brushed along her freckled neck.

"Of course, girl. I'm practically Jones royalty now. And I still live two blocks away," Rose answered easily. She disentangled herself from Ellie to wrap Jolene in a warm embrace of her own.

"It's great to see you, Rose," Jolene said.

"Same here," Rose replied happily.

"Where's your better half?" Ellie asked with a smirk.

Rose pointed across the room.

"She's been talking to that kid over there for, like, ten minutes. I think she's trying to convince her to apply here next year."

"Well, I think everyone in this room could convince her to do that!" Ellie said.

"True. It's not every day you see so many remarkable alums in one place," Rose offered before taking a sip of her wine. "And one standing right in front of me, no less! How does it feel to be a Jones Medal winner?"

Jolene blushed at the attention as Ellie elbowed her through her suit jacket. She could see the pride written clear across her wife's face. She still wasn't used to being recognized for her achievements, but Ellie's delighted expression made it easier to accept.

"It's pretty weird, honestly," she admitted.

"Do you have to give a speech or anything tomorrow?" Rose asked.

"No, thank god," Jolene exhaled. "They just bring all the winners up on stage and talk about us for a minute or two before they hand out the medals. I don't think I could do a speech," she said.

"Oh sure you could!" Ellie interjected.

"I'm sure their introduction will be just fine." Jolene shrugged.

"No, I think I could do better. I already have it planned out," she joked, leaping at the opportunity to wax poetically about her partner.

"Typical," Jolene hummed.

"What?"

"You're still an overachiever," she explained with one eyebrow raised accusingly.

"Let's hear it, then. I'll be the judge to see if it does our Jojo justice," Rose goaded.

Ellie took a deep breath. "Okay, this is how I would introduce you." She dipped into her "announcer voice" and moved her arms to present Jolene like a letter on *Wheel of Fortune*. "May I present Ms. Jolene Gallagher-Weiss, class of 2015 and new recipient of the prestigious Jones Medal! Working tirelessly since her graduation from Jones University, this remarkable woman has proved her mettle in both the political world and the private sector. After, count them, eleven successful campaigns for various senators in DC, she moved on to greener and, let's be honest, less profitable pastures. She left the political sector to start a homeless youth charity, which she now chairs and operates. And, she does all this while juggling her other job as wife to the director of a suitably impressive Smithsonian branch and adoptive mother of two gangly, yet lovable teens." Ellie finished with a breathless flourish. She grabbed her drink out of Jolene's hand and took a satisfied sip while Rose gave a polite golf clap. She cleared her throat.

"I'd give it an eight point five. It could have used more talk about lesbians and friends named Rose. That would have given you a perfect score," she proclaimed with a confident smirk directed at Ellie.

"I'll keep that in mind if they ask me to get up there tomorrow," Ellie answered with a wink. She ran her fingers under Jolene's suit jacket to rest on her lower back.

"Okay, I'm going to go track down my lady and make sure she doesn't need to be saved from that kid. I'll make sure we catch up with you in a bit?" Rose asked.

"Sure. We'll be here," Jolene said.

"Congrats again, Jojo. I'm so proud of you. Both of you!" she added as she walked away. Rose sauntered across the room and Ellie and Jolene giggled together as she made her overbearing presence known in the conversation between her partner and the prospective student.

"I love that woman," Ellie admitted.

"Hey!"

"Obviously I love you too," Ellie said, rolling her eyes.

Jolene reached out and plucked the nearly empty glass from her wife's hand. She put it down on the table beside them and slotted their fingers together.

"Come with me?" Jolene asked quietly.

"Depends where we're going," Ellie answered smoothly.

"Come on."

Jolene led her wife onto the stage, greeting fellow alumnae at the dais from the "Welcome Alumnae!" panel. She navigated through the women and pulled Ellie toward the door that led to the backstage area.

"After you," Jolene urged.

"Are we going where I think we're going?" Ellie asked as she stepped into the dark hallway.

"Yes," Jolene replied.

They walked together, arm in arm, to the end of the hall where they were met by another familiar door. Ellie's memories all flooded back.

"You're making me go back in the closet," she whined with one hand on her hip.

"Only if you want to join me," Jolene offered as she waggled her eyebrows. She opened the door and turned on the light and beckoned her wife to follow her inside.

"It's not very ladylike for a prestigious Jones Medal winner to hook up with someone in a supply closet on the night before the awards presentation," Ellie said nonchalantly. Still, Jolene could see the spark of mischief in her eyes.

"Guess I'm not much of a lady then." She reached out a hand and waited for Ellie to grab hold. After a pause, Ellie linked their fingers. Jolene quickly pulled her into the room and shut the door. She dipped down to kiss Ellie. Their lips had memorized the motions long ago, but that same love and tenderness was still there, etched in every motion and every word they shared together.

"You cried a lot the last time we were in this room," Ellie whispered in between soft kisses.

"I did," Jolene answered breathlessly, "but it was all worth it to be back here again with you."

"You sap," Ellie accused. "I'm going to need a hankie."

"Good news, I happen to have one handy," she answered slyly. Jolene reached into her jacket pocket.

"You've gotta be kidding me."

"Nope."

Ellie looked down to see her old Jones Tones scarf nestled in the hand between them.

"I can't believe this!" she said, a wide grin pulled across her face. "Jesus, where did you find it?"

"I've had it in my desk drawer for years. Just had to wait for the right time to give it back to you," she explained. She handed over the soft fabric. Ellie marveled at the scarf in her hands.

"This brings back a lot of memories."

"Good ones?"

She looked up into her wife's warm eyes.

"Yes," she replied. She reached up the few inches that separated them to kiss Jolene desperately. All of those long-ago struggles had led to this outcome. Of course they were good memories.

Ellie broke away from the heated kiss. Her eyes searched Jolene's face, the tan skin now lined with crow's-feet and a few well-earned wrinkles between her eyebrows. Her hair had lost its black intensity and was threaded with touches of light gray. She spent a moment wondering if Jolene's hair would eventually go completely white. She would be quite a beauty, if that were the case. Either way, Ellie would still be madly in love with the woman in her arms. She touched the braid draped over her wife's shoulder, so different from the one she remembered from their college years. Jolene was a vision of perfection to Ellie, and had been for decades. She breathed a sigh as a slow smile spread across her features.

"What?" Jolene asked.

"I'm glad you're here," she answered.

Jolene felt transported, remembering how Ellie had said those same words a quarter century before in this exact same spot. Her heart warmed at the memory.

"Me too."

Bella Books, Inc.

Women. Books. Even Better Together.

P.O. Box 10543
Tallahassee, FL 32302

Phone: 800-729-4992
www.bellabooks.com